"Could you walk me through what happened?" Jason asked.

"Okay."

Unease crept through her as she reentered the house. Was it from replaying the horrible memory of earlier that night? Or was it because the man walking behind her stood on this same spot thirteen years ago and broke her heart?

She forced herself to stay in the present and went through the events of the evening, showing Jason how she'd come in, where she'd dropped her keys, the light that didn't work in the garage.

Finally, she ran out of words. Someone had tried to kill her tonight. Her home, her haven, her sanctuary had been violated. And now Jason was back.

Oh, Father, how did my life wind up this way?

A gentle tug on her elbow pulled her back to the present. Jason edged between her and the car and looked deep into her eyes. "Caroline." He swallowed hard and tried again. "You have no reason to trust me, or believe me, or even want me around." Regret pierced every word. "But I promise you that I will not stop until we've found out what's going on

HIDDEN LEGACY

LYNN HUGGINS BLACKBURN

HARLEQUIN®LOVE INSPIRED® SUSPENSE

Recycling programs
for this product may
not exist in your area.

LOVE INSPIRED BOOKS

ISBN-13: 978-0-373-21625-3

Hidden Legacy

www.Harlequin.com

Printed in U.S.A.

The fear of man bringeth a snare: but whoso putteth his trust in the Lord shall be safe.
—*Proverbs* 29:25

For Emma—I adore you and am so thankful God chose me to be your mommy. I love you, pumpkin!

Acknowledgments

Never-ending thanks goes to...

Brian—for supporting me every step of the way. None of this would be possible without you. I love you!

Emma, James and Drew—for making every day a real-life adventure.

My parents, sister and in-laws—for being my biggest cheerleaders and for the countless hours of babysitting that made this book possible.

My sisters in the Light Brigade—for your love and friendship, and for praying me through another story.

My critique partners—for talking me through plot points and off ledges.

Retired South Carolina family court judge Kinard Johnson—for gladly answering my rambling questions about wills and custody issues.

Daniel Fetterolf—for answering random questions about police procedures.

Lynette Eason—for so many things, but especially for reading the roughest of rough drafts.

Tamela Hancock Murray—for your guidance and for being a constant source of encouragement.

Elizabeth Mazer—for, once again, making the story so much better.

ONE

The house had been ransacked.

Caroline Harrison squeezed baby Henry closer. Her chest tightened, and each breath came as a spasm as she took in the scene. Chair and sofa cushions lay scattered around the living room. Glass from a shattered vase littered the rug. Two plants had crashed to the floor, their leaves and soil mingled with books yanked from the bookcase.

Who had done this?

Why?

What if they were still here?

A scraping noise from the back of the house answered her silent question. Her skin tingled, and acid filled her mouth.

She had to get out. Now. Her parents' home was a quarter of a mile back down the winding mountain road. Too far to run with a sixteen-month-old in her arms.

She needed to get to her car. Once she got away, she'd call 911 and wait for the police. She backed up, one slow step at a time, reaching into her pocket for her keys.

Keys that weren't there.

She patted the other jacket pocket. Also empty. Panic threatened to overwhelm her, but she kept moving—closing the distance between the den and the garage, where the safety of her car waited.

What had she done with her keys?

Her mind spun, retracing her steps.

She'd pulled into her dark garage, frustrated that the bulbs in the garage door opener had blown out—again. She'd grabbed the diaper bag—

That was it. The keys were in the diaper bag.

She'd dropped the bag on the table by the door as she'd entered. She continued to ease backward toward the garage, taking each step with care. Maybe whoever was inside was so busy stealing something they hadn't noticed her arrival. The longer they stayed occupied, the better her chance of getting away.

Henry slept on, oblivious to the unfolding drama.

Her hand closed around the strap of the overflowing diaper bag. Why hadn't she cleaned it out this morning? If anything fell out on the floor as she made her escape...

She slid the strap over her shoulder and reached behind her with her free hand. She'd find the keys after she got in the car.

She hadn't realized her palms were sweating until she couldn't grip the doorknob. She rubbed her free hand on her pants and tried again. The knob turned without a sound, but as she opened the door, she braced for the chime from her security system that usually alerted her to any opened door or window.

Nothing happened.

The burglar had disabled her alarm. She hurried down the two steps that led into the garage, every cell in her body screaming for her to go faster, every neuron in her brain urging her to move with more caution. She pulled the door behind her, stopping short of closing it all the way.

With her free hand out to keep from crashing into her car, she crept around to the driver's side. She opened the door, and the click of the handle ricocheted around the room. Anyone in the house could have heard that. Or not. Maybe it only seemed loud because she was hyperaware of every sound. Her blood pounded and her breath rasped, despite her best efforts to make no noise. Opening the door activated the car's dome light, and she hit three wrong buttons before she managed to extinguish it. She settled into the seat, sweet Henry still resting on her shoulder.

She couldn't risk opening the back door to strap him into his seat. What if he woke up and started crying? As soon as she was sure they were safe, she'd stop and secure him.

She eased the door closed and fumbled with the diaper bag, digging in the pockets for the keys.

Come on, come on. They had to be here.

Where were they?

Her hand closed over her cell phone, and she grabbed it and punched 911 as she continued to search for her stupid keys. Why, oh why, hadn't she purchased the car with the keyless ignition? It had seemed like such a pointless feature at the time. She'd give anything for it now.

"911, what's your emergency?" The operator's voice echoed through the car.

"My name is Caroline Harrison," she whispered. "I live at 2200 Mountain View Drive. My home has been broken into. I think the person is still in the house."

"Where are you now?"

"In my car in the garage, but I can't find my keys."

"I'm sending someone now. We have a unit not far from you."

"Tell them to hurry!"

"Stay on the line with me, Ms. Harrison."

"I'll try."

"Are you alone?"

"No. I have my...my...son." She didn't have

time to explain the complicated relationship she had with this sweet child. And he *was* her son. It would be official in two weeks.

"How old is he?"

"Sixteen months."

Finally!

Her fingers wrapped around the keys. She shoved the diaper bag into the passenger seat and rested the keys on her leg, tracing each one in the dark to find the car key.

Her hands shook and she pulled in a triumphant breath when she slid the right one in the ignition. She didn't turn it yet—didn't want the noise of the engine to alert her intruder. She'd make sure she was ready to exit first.

She reached for the button on her visor that would activate the garage door opener, but the door into the house opened. She bit back a scream as a man's silhouette appeared and stalked toward her.

"There's someone here."

"I'm sorry, Ms. Harrison, I didn't quite catch that. Did you say there was someone—"

"He's coming—"

She was out of time. No sense in hiding now. She reached for the garage door opener again. She wasn't going to sit here and wait for him to do whatever he planned to do.

She pressed the button. Again. And again. Why wasn't it opening?

The horrible truth overwhelmed her. He must have known she was in here. While she'd thought she was getting away undetected, he'd managed to disable her garage door. Probably flipped the breaker in the laundry room. There was no way her little Camry could drive through the garage door, but she had to try.

She turned the key. In the light filtering in from the house, she saw the gun in his hand.

He aimed it at her window.

Detective Jason Drake pulled his Ford Explorer into the restaurant parking lot and answered his cell phone. "Hey, Michael. I'm here," he said. He and Michael Ellis had met for dinner almost every Thursday night since he'd come to work for the Henderson County Sheriff's Office six months ago.

"Sorry, man. I'm not going to make it. Dispatch called."

"Like that's a surprise," Jason said. It had taken him all of two days on the job to realize his old friend had a soft spot for the dispatcher.

"It's not like that," Michael said. "We got a call from the Harrisons."

The Harrisons. He fought the memories pounding on the door of his heart. "Is something wrong at the plant?"

"No. The call came from Caroline Harrison."

The mention of her name opened the floodgates, and memories engulfed him. Big blue eyes flashing in laughter at a private joke. Full lips curved into a smile that was only for him. The many times he'd held her hand. The one time he'd held her in his arms.

"She said there was an armed intruder at her house."

Jason floored it. "I'm on my way."

His phone rang one minute later. The sheriff.

"Drake, we have a situation at Caroline Harri—"

Despite his respect for his boss, Jason cut the man off. "Yes, sir, I heard."

"I want you to take the lead on this."

Good. Now he had an excuse to be there. Not that it would have mattered. He had to make sure Caroline was all right.

"Of course, sir. I'm on my way."

"Jason, I want this case solved fast, you hear me? And I want you to do whatever you have to do to keep Caroline Harrison safe."

"Yes, sir."

It took five agonizing minutes to reach the Harrisons' gated driveway. One uniformed officer stood there, blocking the path up the mountain.

Jason rolled down his window and the young man—Dan? Dave? He'd figure it out later—approached his window.

"Hey, Jason. You here for the excitement, too, huh? It's a madhouse up there."

Jason could sense the kid's disappointment

about not being more directly involved, but he didn't have time to play nice with… Dalton. That was it. "What's the status?"

"The house is secure. Caroline and the baby are fine, just shook up. No idea where the intruder is."

"Thanks." He started to roll up the window.

"Hey." Dalton put a hand out. "You know where you're going, right? Caroline's place is past the senior Harrisons' about a quarter of a mile."

He knew. This driveway was one long memory. He drove past the short drive to the house where her brother, Blake, lived with his daughter and his new wife, Heidi. He hadn't had a chance to meet her yet.

As he approached Caroline's parents' home, the activity level increased. Officers and patrol cars with lights flashing dotted the mountain. The house glowed like a beacon. He'd spent so many happy hours in that house. Jeffrey and Eleanor had always welcomed him. Until he blew it with Caroline.

He forced his mind back to the present.

Dwelling on the mistakes of the past wouldn't change anything.

He followed the driveway past the Harrisons' home and farther up the mountain. They'd hiked to the top of this mountain more than once, and Caroline always said this was where she wanted to live. At sixteen, she hadn't been sure her dad would sell her the land.

Of course, Jeffrey Harrison had done one better. Jason could still remember the excitement in his mom's voice as she'd filled him in. "Caroline stopped by last week," she'd said. "She's so excited. Jeffrey and Eleanor gave her the top of the mountain for her twenty-fifth birthday. She's meeting with an architect this week and planning her dream house."

He eased around a final curve. Dream house, indeed.

She'd always been fond of stonework, and the house blended seamlessly into the mountain. Positioned as it was, the views from the deck would be breathtaking, but only one view captured his mind.

Caroline Harrison.

Even after all this time, he couldn't look at her without seeing his long-lost best friend. If only he could erase that night. That one conversation. That one kiss that had ruined everything. If he'd kept his mouth shut…

No. It had been the right decision then. Still was. Still hurt.

He stepped from the car and made his way through the throng of first responders, most of whom he knew were off duty. He couldn't fault them. Armed intruders weren't part of the daily grind in Etowah, North Carolina.

He stepped into the glow shining from floodlights, and she looked into his eyes.

"Jason."

It was the first time she'd willingly spoken to him in thirteen years, and in her voice he heard a whisper of hope. Not hope for the future they could never have. But maybe hope for the forgiveness he did not deserve.

She offered him a wavering smile. "I'm glad you're here."

An olive branch? "Me, too." He stared into

her eyes a few moments longer than he should have. So many things needed to be said, but they would have to wait. Michael and a young officer were headed their way.

"Heard you'd been assigned the case," Michael said.

"Yeah. Bring me up to speed."

TWO

Caroline half listened as they filled Jason in.

"Responded to the call at 7:12… Shots fired… Neither Caroline nor Henry was hurt… Caroline said he took off when he heard the sirens."

At that line, his eyes flicked in her direction and then lingered. Jason's face twisted with an expression she couldn't read. Was he angry? Frustrated? Amused? She chewed on her inner lip. She used to be able to read his face from across a classroom and know exactly what he was thinking.

"We've checked the property as much as we can in the dark. We'll be back out here in the morning to look for tracks."

"Security system?"

"Like nothing I've ever seen. But the intruder managed to disable it."

Jason turned to her. "What's the story on your security?"

"I don't know much about it other than that it's high-tech. Heidi, my sister-in-law, had it installed. She's an FBI agent." Jason didn't seem as surprised as she'd expected him to be. So, his mom had been filling him in over the years. She should have figured. Their moms had been friends for twenty-five years. She suspected they held out hope that she and Jason would kiss and make up.

Not likely.

The kissing was what had messed up everything to begin with.

Michael's phone rang. He apologized and stepped away to answer it. Jason turned to the other officer, clapping him on the shoulder. "Good work tonight." The officer, who couldn't be more than twenty-three, stood taller under his praise.

"Thank you, sir." He nodded at Caroline. "Ma'am."

When he walked away, she looked at Jason. "Ma'am? Really? I'm not that old."

He gave her another look she couldn't decipher. "No, you aren't. But he is that young." He glanced around. "Where's Henry?"

Caroline pointed toward the house. "He fell asleep as soon as the EMTs were done checking us out," she said. "One of the officers gave me permission to lay him down in the pack 'n' play. He can sleep through anything."

Jason smiled. "I want to meet him, but I guess that will have to wait. Could you walk me through what happened?"

"Okay."

Unease crept through her as she reentered the house. Was it from replaying the horrible memory of earlier that night? Or was it because the man walking behind her stood on this same spot thirteen years ago and broke her heart as he swore he'd never waste his life living in this little town? Nothing she could say had convinced him to stay. Even when she'd told him how she felt... Her skin warmed in the cool evening air. That was a long time ago. She'd been young. She'd been stupid.

She was neither of those things anymore.

She forced herself to stay in the present and went through the events of the evening, showing Jason how she'd come in, where she'd dropped her keys, the light that didn't work in the garage.

When she got back to her car, she ran out of words. Someone had tried to kill her tonight. Her home, her haven, her sanctuary had been violated. And now, Jason was back.

Oh, Father, how did my life wind up this way?

She didn't know how long she stared at her car—a still-life metaphor for her messed-up world.

A gentle tug on her elbow pulled her back to the present. Jason edged between her and the car and looked deep into her eyes. This time, she had no difficulty understanding the emotion she saw there. She'd recognize that look of determination anywhere.

"Caroline." He swallowed hard and tried again. "You have no reason to trust me, or believe me, or even want me around." Regret pierced every word. "But I promise you I will not stop until we've found out what's going on."

Caroline noted that he hadn't said they'd catch the guy. She'd learned that much from Heidi. No matter what branch they were in, the really good law enforcement officers never made a promise they couldn't keep. Still, there was comfort in his intensity.

"Thank you, Jason."

He smiled and quirked an eyebrow at her. "Mom says you come by at least once a month."

She would have appreciated the change of subject if it had been anything else. Were they going to talk about this now? Keep it light, she chanted to herself. "I like your mom." She forced a smile. "Of course, I can't go by more often. I gain five pounds every time I walk in the door."

Jason patted his stomach. "Tell me about it. I'm having to put in a couple extra miles every day now."

"You poor thing." Caroline didn't try to veil the sarcasm.

"I don't want to hurt her feelings by not eating a slice of pie every night. And then for breakfast."

Caroline couldn't stop the laughter that bubbled out. "You're a good son," she said. Jason laughed with her, and for a moment the fear lost its grip on her heart.

Jason leaned against the car. "But why do you do it? I doubt you visit all your high school friends' parents."

So much for keeping it light. Surely he hadn't forgotten the promise she'd made—thirteen years ago—to keep an eye on his folks when he left for the Marine Corps. "You know why."

She could see it on his face. He knew. So why ask? What had he been fishing for?

He walked to the front of the car and studied the bullet hole in her windshield. "I guess it's just nice to know that some things never change."

"True. That's why I wasn't surprised to hear that you were coming home. I knew you would," she said.

Jason's eyes met hers, sadness mingled with confusion.

"I'm sorry about your dad, Jason."

She saw the muscles in his neck tighten. "Thanks," he said, then cleared his throat. "Me, too."

Another throat cleared nearby. Michael Ellis nodded at her. "We're done in the house, Caroline. Thought you might want to put Henry in his crib."

"Thanks, Michael. I appreciate that."

Michael turned to Jason. "When you get a minute, we need to talk."

Something in his tone sent a shudder through Caroline's system. "If it's about me, my house, my child or the man who tried to kill me tonight, why don't you go ahead and say what you need to say?"

Michael's eyes darted from Caroline's face to Jason's. It wouldn't take a body language expert to read his silent plea for help.

"Caroline, if I promise to tell you everything, will you give me fifteen minutes to wrap things up? It would be easier if I can send as many of these guys home as possible. Then we can talk without being interrupted."

Oh, how she wanted to argue. She knew Jason had thrown in the part about letting the others go home because it would play on her sympathies. The worst part was, he was right.

"Fine. Talk. Send people home. Then I want to hear everything. Tonight."

Michael didn't try to hide his relief.

Jason held her gaze. "I promise."

Jason couldn't deny he enjoyed seeing the feisty side of Caroline Harrison. "Why don't you go inside? Grab something to drink. Get away from the chaos. I'll finish up and be with you soon."

Her eyes still held a hint of challenge. "*Soon* doesn't mean an hour from now, Jason Drake."

"Yes, ma'am." She glared at him before she turned and walked away. He was glad to see the show of spirit, all the more because he could tell she was shaken. She kept chewing on her lip. She probably didn't realize that she was clenching and unclenching her hands as she talked. Or that she'd been rocking back and forth on her heels.

But she wasn't falling apart. Not that he was surprised. Caroline Harrison was a rock. Always had been. Some things really didn't change.

And some things did. Like him—back in town after he'd made it clear to her and everyone else that he would never return here. Could never live his life in this place. Not because it wasn't beautiful or because he didn't love his family.

Well, the family he claimed, anyway.

But the father he *didn't* choose to claim— the biological parent who had made a misery of Jason's childhood, and whom Jason had been thrilled to replace with a loving, honorable stepfather—lived here, too. He kept calling. Probably to express his disapproval of Jason's career choices. Again.

He shoved the thoughts away. He had much bigger things to worry about right now. Like figuring out who would want to kill Caroline.

It took Jason thirty minutes to speak with

Michael and wrap things up with the officers who'd converged on Caroline's home. He wasn't surprised to have multiple volunteers to provide a protective detail for the evening.

"Dalton and Michael, you guys take the watch tonight. We'll decide if we need some sort of rotation for the rest of the week later."

Dalton was inexperienced but energetic enough to stay awake after all the excitement died down. Michael was solid. If any trouble broke out, he'd be able to handle it.

Content that things were well in hand, he walked up the steps to Caroline's front door. Should he knock? The place had been swarming with police officers and crime scene techs all evening, but now that things had quieted, he hated to be intrusive.

He tapped on the door and eased it open. "Caroline? You okay in there?"

"I'm good. Just getting Henry settled for the night. Come on in."

Jason closed the door behind him. Caroline stood in the hallway with a drowsy Henry in her arms, his little head nestled on her shoulder, eyes half-shut. She shifted him gently, her cheek resting on the top of his head. "Give me a moment," she said in a whisper.

Motherhood suited her. He refused to dwell on the regret trying to surface. She'd never been his. They'd never had a future. She was a natural as a mother, but he had no plans to find out what kind of father he would be. He couldn't risk being as terrible at it as the men in his own genetic family tree.

Caroline disappeared down the hall, and Jason looked around the ravaged living room again. Who would do this? Break-ins happened, but this seemed like more. His fingers curled into fists. He'd find the person who did this one way or another.

Caroline returned a minute later. "So, what did Michael tell you that has you all riled up?"

"I'll answer, but I need to ask a few questions first."

She glared at him.

"I wouldn't be doing my job if I didn't consider all the possibilities."

"Fine. Can I start cleaning up this mess while we talk?"

"Of course. I'll help." Caroline had always been a neat freak. Another thing that hadn't changed. He pulled a throw pillow from the floor and tossed it onto the sofa. Caroline grabbed a blanket he recognized. Her grandmother had crocheted it for her years ago. She hugged it to her chest for a brief moment before she folded it and draped it over the corner of the sofa.

"Is there anyone in your life who would want to hurt you?"

"No."

"What about at work? A disgruntled employee?" Caroline had an important upper-management position in her family's company. If someone was unhappy at the plant, she'd be a visible target for their frustrations.

"No."

"I'm going to need more than one-word answers."

She huffed and righted an orchid that had been dumped on the floor. "Fine. No issues at work. I handle the finances, and I'm taking on more of the personnel responsibilities as Dad is turning over more control to Blake and me. But we haven't fired anyone in years. Everyone is getting paid on time. No one is complaining. I can't fathom anyone from HPI doing something like this."

Harrison Plastics International had always been the place everyone in town wanted to work. Didn't sound like anything had changed there.

"What about suppliers? Clients? Anyone unhappy?"

Caroline rolled her head from one side to the other. Was there someone unhappy? "What are you thinking?"

She placed the plant on the end table. "We've made a few changes recently. A new paper product vendor. A new printer lease. Blake changed a major raw material supplier. But nothing that would cause anyone to try to shoot me."

He'd talk to Blake. Caroline's brother had

always been protective of his little sister. Which was probably why he hadn't been particularly fond of Jason. But he might have a different perspective than Caroline on this subject.

"Where is Blake? For that matter, where is everybody?"

"What do you mean?"

"Your parents? Blake, Heidi and Maggie? I'm surprised we don't have an entire contingent of the FBI here."

Caroline scooped a handful of books from the floor. "Mom and Dad are on a mission trip to a refugee camp in Greece."

"Didn't your dad have a stroke a couple of years ago?"

"He did, but he's made a full recovery."

"That's great." He heard the wistfulness in his words. There would be no happy ending for his own dad. ALS would take his life, one agonizing piece at a time. "That explains where your parents are. What about Blake, Heidi and Maggie?"

"Blake and Maggie are on a father/daughter mission trip. They support a family in Haiti and went down over spring break with a group from the church. They'll be back next week."

"And Heidi is off doing something mysterious?"

"Exactly."

He studied a family photo on her mantel. "Tell me about your new sister-in-law."

"Heidi does a lot of undercover work. That's what brought her here last year. That's how she and Blake met. So sometimes she's gone. Not as much as she used to be, and usually not for more than a day or two. I don't know if Blake even knows what she does or where she goes."

She brushed some fingerprint dust off the upright piano. "I'm going to need to try to find her, though. She's the only one who understands the security system."

"Why her?"

"When we had that trouble at the plant—I'm assuming your mom told you about that?"

"Oh, yeah." His mom had bent his ear for three hours that night. After he'd joined the sheriff's department, he'd learned the whole story. The one that had somehow never fully been told in the press. Heidi's team, with Blake's assistance, had prevented a nationwide anthrax outbreak.

"Heidi revamped all the security systems here and at the plant. We have motion detectors, cameras, safe rooms and probably a bunch of other stuff I don't even know about. It's not an out-of-the-box system. It doesn't have a local monitoring station, although it is monitored somewhere. Maybe in DC? It has Department of Defense–level encryption. Very hard to hack."

"Is it possible you forgot to turn it on before you left this morning?"

"No."

"Are you sure?"

"Positive."

"How can you know? I forget stuff all the time."

She smirked at him. "I remember because Henry was screaming his head off and I was singing to him as I punched in the code."

That sounded like a solid memory, unfortunately. The idea that this highly advanced system had been on when the intruder arrived worried him because it meant the intruder knew how to turn it *off*. So either they were dealing with a tech expert way beyond the typical, garden-variety thief, or the intruder was someone she knew and trusted. He wasn't sure which possibility was worse.

But either way, she deserved to know what they were dealing with.

"From what you described to me," he said, "it doesn't sound like the security system was on when you got home. Who else knows the code? A housekeeper, maybe?" He took a deep breath. "Boyfriend?"

She shot him a withering look. "I have a

full-time job and a baby. Romance isn't a high priority these days."

Jason didn't bother to process why her words sent a wave of relief crashing through his soul.

"What about Julia? Does she still clean for you?"

The Harrisons' housekeeper had always been gracious to him as a kid.

"Yes, but I change the code every week. She calls me when she gets here, and I give her the new code."

"You change the code every week?"

"Heidi is a stickler about it. I change it every Sunday night."

The weight of her words hit him hard. "Caroline, whoever this guy is, he was able to come inside and disable your security system. We have to consider the possibility that he is highly skilled and he's been watching you and your family and knew you were up here alone tonight."

Caroline's hand shook as she reached for

her glass and took a sip. "So this wasn't a random attack. You think he was targeting me on purpose."

"Right. And he may not be done."

THREE

The knock at the door startled Caroline. The way Jason's hand flew to the gun at his waist told her it had caught him off guard, as well.

"Open up." Hearing Michael's voice put Caroline at ease, but Jason didn't remove his hand from his weapon.

"You didn't answer your phone, man," Michael called. "We had the guys grab sub sandwiches, and if you don't like what's on yours, you have no one to blame but yourself. Open up."

It was almost ten o'clock. He hadn't eaten? Her cheeks burned with the realization that coming to her rescue had interrupted his evening plans. "I'm so sorry. You should have told me."

He waved her off. "I had a candy bar. I'm fine."

He opened the door, and Michael held out a cellophane bag. "Got you a club. There's a bag of chips in there, too." He smiled at Caroline. "Don't worry about anything tonight. Dalton and I will keep a close eye on things."

"Wha—"

"Thanks, man. I'll talk to you in a little while." Jason closed the door on the still-smiling Michael before he could say another word.

"What was he talking about?"

"Just a precaution. You're up here alone with Henry and—"

"And someone knows how to get into my house."

Jason studied the contents of his bag instead of replying.

"Fine," she said. "Let's sit down in the kitchen. You eat, and we'll catch up on the last thirteen years."

"Mind if I wash up first?"

Caroline pointed out the bathroom door and walked into her kitchen. When the click of the door reached her ears, she slid onto a bar stool.

What was happening? *Why* was it happening? And why did Jason Drake have to be the one responsible for her case?

Jason.

Part of her longed to have him sitting beside her. Shoulders touching, feet propped up on the coffee table—the way they'd watched hours of Duke basketball games in their teens.

Part of her wanted to kick him out and tell him to stay away forever.

It wouldn't be easy, but it could be done. She'd been doing it quite successfully for the past few months. She'd avoided him, and any mention of him.

Why should she hide from him, though? She hadn't done anything wrong, and she had nothing to apologize for. The way things had ended between them was embarrassing, but surely he couldn't think she still had feelings for him. What happened was ancient history. And if the sheriff thought he was the best person to close this case, then she had to trust in that. She couldn't take any risks when it came to her safety or Henry's.

"Caroline, are you okay?"

Her stomach somersaulted at his voice. Ancient history or current event?

No. She'd learned her lesson. Jason Drake had been a fabulous friend, but he'd made it clear he wanted nothing more. "I'm fine." She pointed him to a seat at the table. "Let me get you some tea." History shouldn't be repeated. For tonight, she'd be thankful she had a friend looking out for her. For the future, she'd remember to look out for herself.

Jason sat, and she didn't miss the weariness on his face as he bowed his head in thanks.

When he lifted his head, he didn't hesitate. "I still have a lot of questions," he admitted.

"What do you want to know?"

Jason swallowed. "Let's start with Henry."

Or course he would want to know about Henry. "I'm surprised your mom hasn't given you all the details."

He took a drink of his tea. "She's given me some of them. What she couldn't explain to me was how you wound up with Stephanie's baby boy."

"I'm still trying to figure that out, myself." She straightened the fringe on her place mat. "Stephanie and I didn't always agree, but we stayed close after high school. She was going to be my maid of honor."

The memory of those days after Chad's death tugged at the edges of Caroline's mind. They would always be dark, but they no longer held the power to suck her into despair. Now they brought deep sadness and the ever-present question of what might have been.

Jason held her eyes. "I was sorry to hear about what happened to your fiancé, Caroline."

"Thank you." What else could she say? When Jason left, she'd moved on, and then the only man who could have possibly blotted out the memory of Jason had been taken too soon by a drunken driver. The idea that it was better to have loved and lost than never to have loved at all came to mind. At this point, she wasn't so sure about that.

And what happened when the one you lost came back?

She shook off the direction of her thoughts. "I finished school, came home and went to work for Dad. Stephanie went to work at the bank and got transferred out to the coast three years ago. We kept in touch, sporadically. A year later, she came home one weekend, and I knew things were different."

Caroline remembered everything about that night. The garlic butter dripping onto the tablecloth, the exact shade of terra-cotta red that rimmed the pasta bowl, the opera music that filtered into the restaurant. And Stephanie. Fidgety. Eyes too bright. A smile that threatened to break into a goofy grin at any moment. "She'd gotten married. Said it was a civil ceremony and she was sorry she hadn't told me earlier. A month later, she was pregnant and making plans to move to the Midwest with her Prince Charming."

Jason pulled a few Doritos from the bag. "Mom told me she came home pregnant and no one ever talks about the baby's father."

"That's an accurate statement," she said. "My phone rang one day, and she told me she was home to stay. She wasn't even showing yet, but it wasn't long before tongues were wagging. She categorically refused to talk about the father. She never even wanted me to tell anyone she'd been married."

Jason's face registered confusion. "Why not?"

"I assumed she was so embarrassed by her choice of husband that she'd rather have people think she'd gotten pregnant out of wedlock."

"Do you think she left her husband to protect the baby or herself?" Jason's voice was cold and hard. "I could respect that."

No doubt he could. He'd been the baby in that situation once. "She never had one negative thing to say about her husband. I asked her if he'd hurt her, but she was adamant that he hadn't. Then she begged me not to ask any more questions."

"I'm guessing you did what she asked." Jason finished off the last bite of his sandwich and tossed the wrappings in the trash.

Had she done the right thing by agreeing to Stephanie's request? Doubts clawed at her heart. "What else could I do?"

"Nothing," Jason said.

She didn't bother to process why that one word sent a shot of relief through her system.

Caroline took a sip of tea. "We almost never spoke of him. Then one night she asked me if I could come over. When I got there, she was a mess. Told me her husband had been killed. She wouldn't share any details, but she was devastated."

"You think she loved him?"

"Yes. At least I'll be able to tell Henry that much."

"What do you mean?"

"I don't know who his father was. Stephanie always referred to him as Lee, and she never changed her last name. His name isn't on the birth certificate."

"Caroline, I have to ask. Do you think Stephanie was ever married? It could have been a one-night stand, and she was embarrassed to admit she didn't know the guy."

"No, I believe there was a real relationship and she did love him. But the rest of the
story—well, I don't know what to believe anymore. Do you… Do you think he might be the
reason someone came after me?"

Jason didn't answer—which was answer
enough. She could put together the logic herself. If someone was targeting her, it was probably connected to the only new element in
her life—her son. And since she knew nothing about his father's family or what trouble
they might bring, she had no idea how to keep
Henry safe.

Jason put one hand on hers. She didn't pull
away, and the softness of her skin threatened
to distract him. He focused on her face. "This
guy, Lee, sounds like a pretty shady character. He could have been married or some type
of criminal…"

"I know."

They sat in silence. He wished he could read
her mind. Was she angry with him for asking

these questions? "I'm surprised your sister-in-law hasn't done some investigating."

"She wanted to, but I begged her to leave it alone. I have a feeling she's been doing some digging on the side, but my guess is she hasn't found anything yet. Besides, she and her partner, Max, have been deep into something lately. That's where she is now—undercover somewhere. When things slow down, I have a feeling she'll start asking a lot more questions."

She dropped her head into her hands. "Maybe I should have taken her up on the offer."

"There's no point in stressing about that now," Jason said. "Let's focus on what we know. How old was Henry when Steph died?" Jason asked.

"Eight months. Car crash. Stephanie died at the scene. Henry got out with barely a scratch. I was listed as her emergency contact. When I went to her place to try to find her insurance information for Henry, I found her will."

"And that's when you found out you'd been named Henry's guardian."

"Yep."

"Must have been a shock."

"You could say that. One minute I was single and unattached. The next I had an eight-month-old to rear."

"Were there any legal challenges?"

He'd been the pawn in a legal battle for a good part of his childhood. It wouldn't surprise him if someone caused trouble without really thinking of Henry's best interests at all.

"No. She had a trust set up for Henry. No one disputed it. There's no mention of the father, beyond the request that I never allow Henry to know that side of his family or for the family to know him." She picked up one of the napkins Jason had left on the table and started folding it into small squares. "Once the chaos settled, I started all the legal proceedings to make sure Stephanie's wishes would be carried out. Her dad has had two heart attacks, and her mom has her hands full taking care of him. They had no interest in contesting the guardianship. The adoption will be final in two weeks."

"Two weeks?"

There was a tone in Jason's voice that Caroline's nerves reverberated to. "Why?"

"The timing of this makes me very suspicious."

"You mean someone who knew the father—"

"Or maybe the father himself? We don't even know if he's dead. Do we?"

Caroline gulped. "No. I guess we don't. But I know this. Henry is mine now, and I'm never letting him go."

Jason heard the mama-bear growl in her voice. He pitied the fool who messed with her on a good day. Raw from the evening's trauma and the past few months of upheaval, Caroline Harrison looked like a woman who wouldn't tolerate any more nonsense.

"The adoption will be final in two weeks and he'll be mine forever." She raked her hands through her hair. "Assuming we're still alive." Caroline placed a bag of Oreos on the table. "Want some milk?"

"Of course I do."

She grinned at him before returning to the fridge. "I knew it. Like I said, some things never change."

She poured two glasses of milk and twisted her Oreo in half. He dunked his in his milk before popping it in his mouth whole.

He needed to ask her one more question. And it had nothing to do with the case. "There's one more thing," he said.

She looked at him over the edge of an Oreo. "Yes?"

"I need to apologize for what I said that night."

Her face flushed. "Maybe we should just pretend that night never happened," she said in a whisper.

Pretend it never happened? He relived it almost every day. "Is that what you've done?" He hated the huskiness in his voice and cleared his throat.

She bit her lip. "You made your feelings pretty clear, Jason. I've always regretted trying to change your mind. I lost so much that night. If I had a time machine, I'd stop my-self from messing things up for both of us."

He swallowed hard. It was now or never. "I've regretted that night for the past thirteen years, as well. But I think for different rea-sons. You spoke from your heart and told the truth."

Spit it out, Drake. "But I didn't. I was afraid. And stupid. I thought I was doing the best thing for both of us, and I'm not convinced that I was wrong about that. But I have regret-ted hurting you every day since." He'd regret-ted it all the more because he'd been in love with her but had been too afraid to tell her, too certain that all the obstacles between them would ruin their chances, and that he'd be bet-ter off not risking his heart or her happiness.

His phone rang, and he ignored it. It rang again. "You'd better get that," she said.

He checked the screen. The sheriff. "Ex-cuse me," he said and walked outside to fill his boss in on the investigation. When he re-turned, Caroline was starting the dishwasher.

"I'm going to join Michael and Dalton outside. If you need anything—"

"Oh, no, you will not," she said. "I've already talked to Michael. He and Dalton have things under control. You need to go home. Tell your folks what's going on. Set their minds at ease."

Apparently their conversation from earlier was over. He watched her set the alarm, although he had to wonder if it would do any good.

"Good night, Caroline," he said.

"Good night, Jason." She closed the door, and the clicking lock pierced his heart. She didn't want him to stay. Just tonight? Or ever?

FOUR

The blare of his phone jolted him from sleep hours later.

The clock said 7:12. The ringtone was the one he'd programmed in last night for Caroline's number.

"Caroline?"

A muffled sound came through the speakers. He grabbed his jeans from the floor and tried to pull them on and not disconnect the call.

"Caroline?" This time the sound was clearer, though it was no less confusing. Was she throwing up?

"Jason," she said, her voice raw and trembling. "Jason, something's wrong. It's Henry! He won't wake up."

Another round of retching followed as he

scrambled to pull on his shoes. He grabbed his service weapon, his badge and his keys. As he unlocked the door to his Explorer, Caroline's agonized voice burst through the phone.

"Come on, Henry. Please. Wake up!"

A crash followed her words. Then silence.

"Caroline!"

Father, protect her.

"Caroline!" She didn't respond. The line was still open. He couldn't bear to disconnect, but had she called 911? Was anyone else on the way? Why had she called him instead of Michael or Dalton?

He put the phone on speaker and grabbed the radio. He called the dispatcher, requesting an ambulance and backup. Then he called out to Michael and Dalton and told them to get in the house even if they had to break down the doors.

In the months since he'd returned to North Carolina, he'd been frustrated by his home's nearness to the Harrisons'. Every time he drove past her driveway he knew he should call her. Every time he didn't he felt guilty.

But this morning, he was thankful to be at the gate in two minutes. He punched in the code she'd given him last night and set the delay on the gate to keep it open for ten minutes. That should be long enough for the ambulance to get here before it closed. Then he sped up the drive. There was no unusual activity at Blake and Heidi's. Nothing at Jeffrey and Eleanor's, either.

He pulled up to her front door, slammed on the brakes and raced to the porch. The door stood open, and he could hear an ambulance screaming its way toward them for the second time in less than twenty-four hours.

"Caroline?"

"Back here," Michael's voice came from the hallway that led to Caroline's room. "I think she passed out. I can't get her to come to. The baby is breathing, but I can't wake him up, either."

Jason knelt by Caroline. Her face was ashen. Her breathing shallow. Michael was alternating between checking on her and Henry, while Dalton was fighting with the blinds on the window.

"Dalton, what are you doing, man?" Jason asked.

"Trying to get this stupid window open. I've seen this before."

"Seen what?"

"Carbon monoxide poisoning. You said Caroline was throwing up, right? And the baby is out? It's textbook."

He was right. "Forget the windows. Let's get them outside." Dalton moved toward Caroline. "I've got her. Michael, get Henry," Jason said. "Babies are most at risk."

Dalton looked worried. "He doesn't have a coat."

"The cold isn't our biggest problem right now," Jason said. "Get him outside!"

He scooped Caroline into his arms and raced to the porch, Michael on his heels, holding Henry. As they stepped onto the porch, he could hear Dalton explaining the situation to the EMTs.

They didn't mess around. They checked

Caroline and Henry for CO levels. It took no time at all to determine they'd both been exposed to dangerous amounts. As an EMT strapped Henry into a harness on the gurney, another held an oxygen mask over his face.

Jason hovered near the chaise where Caroline lay on the front porch. Her eyes fluttered open and she clutched at his arm. "Where—"

The words were cut off as her body heaved. She turned away from him, and vomit hit the porch. All he could do was rub her back as violent shudders tore through her.

"Henry!" she gasped.

Jason held on to her. "It's carbon monoxide, Caroline. They're giving him oxygen."

A flurry of activity caught his eye.

"Hey, little man's coming around!" The young EMT didn't try to hide her joy. "That's right, Henry. It's okay, buddy."

"Hear that, Caroline? He's waking up."

"I want to see him," she said, struggling to her feet.

"Whoa," Jason said. "Do you think you can walk?" He scrambled around the chaise and put an arm around her. She was so focused on Henry, she didn't seem to notice the condition of her pajamas. Her pants and T-shirt were flecked with the remains of her stomach's contents.

He held her tight as she shuffled toward the ambulance. "Are you sure—"

"I'm fine."

He had to admit, for someone who'd been puking her guts out two minutes earlier, and unconscious three minutes before that, she seemed remarkably steady on her feet.

Michael and Dalton hovered near the gurney where little Henry was blinking groggily.

"Hey, baby," Caroline said.

One of the EMTs took her arm. "Ms. Harrison, how are you feeling?"

Jason released her to the EMT and motioned Dalton and Michael over to the side.

"Did either of you see anything suspicious last night?"

"No. We walked around the house twenty times at least," Dalton said.

Michael smirked. "Yeah, so we wouldn't fall asleep."

Jason couldn't fault them for that.

"Dalton," Jason said, tossing him the keys to his car. "Trunk. Grab the duffel bag."

The kid ran in the direction of his car.

"What are you thinking, Michael?"

"Besides that you've got puke all over you and don't seem to care?"

"Besides that."

"Well, if that's off the table, then I'm thinking maybe we know what our intruder was up to when he broke in last night. Since Caroline confirmed nothing was taken, we knew it hadn't been a robbery. This might have been what he was after all along."

"Yeah. That's what I'm thinking, too."

Dalton ran up with his go bag.

"Thanks, Dalton."

"Sure thing."

Jason peeked around the corner of the ambulance door as they loaded the gurney with Henry on it into the back of the ambulance.

Caroline took a seat beside the gurney, and they strapped an oxygen mask to her face.

Jason patted her knee. "I'll be right behind you."

As the ambulance pulled away, Jason turned to Dalton and Michael. "I'm going to change. There's no way this place doesn't have at least one CO detector. Find them. Or find where they used to be."

"Think they're defective, boss?" Dalton asked.

"Something like that," he said.

Caroline held Henry's hand with one hand and her oxygen mask with the other as they made their way to the hospital.

Carbon monoxide poisoning?

How?

She had smoke detectors, carbon monoxide detectors, motion detectors and who knew what other types of detectors, thanks to Heidi.

How could this have happened?

She looked at her pants. Then her shirt. Oh, no.

"It's okay, Ms. Harrison," the EMT said as she handed her a towel.

"It's Caroline."

"Hi, Caroline. I'm Lucy."

Caroline tried to wipe away the worst of the spots.

"Vomiting is a good sign," Lucy said. "It means your exposure level isn't so bad that it's started to affect your brain function."

Caroline appreciated Lucy's effort to make her feel better.

"It may be a good sign, but I'd really like some clean clothes," she said.

Lucy adjusted the oxygen mask on Henry's face. "I'm sure that cute cop will bring you some. Is he your boyfriend?"

Lucy's words unleashed a new horror.

Jason. She'd thrown up in front of Jason. Why had she called Jason?

She knew why.

He'd programmed his number into her phone last night. Tested it before he left so it was the last number dialed and the first one to pop up when she'd frantically grabbed it.

But that wasn't really why.

She'd called him because she knew he would take care of it. Take care of *her*. That despite the past thirteen years of awkwardness, he would come when she called.

He'd come.

And found her covered in vomit.

She glanced at her clothes again. Correction. Pajamas. The Duke pajamas she'd gotten for Christmas her senior year of high school, right after she was accepted.

She dropped her head into her free hand.

"You okay, Caroline?" Lucy's concern popped her head back up.

"I threw up in front of him," she said.

Lucy smirked. "He didn't seem to mind."

Caroline groaned.

"Don't worry," Lucy said. "We'll get you some scrubs to put on when we get to the hospital."

"Thanks."

Caroline tried to pull her mind back to more pressing issues. Like how had this happened? Why?

What kind of sick person would be willing to kill a baby?

Because there was one thing she was sure of.

This hadn't been an accident.

Thirty minutes later, Caroline rested on the hospital bed in the small emergency department room. Lucy had come through with the scrubs. Henry was curled beside her wrapped in a tiny hospital gown. Both of them still wore their oxygen masks, but their CO levels had dropped significantly. The doctor had indicated he would run a few tests, but they'd probably be able to go home in a few hours.

"Knock, knock," Jason's soft voice preceded his head peering around the door. A smile lit his features. "You look so much better," he said.

"Thanks a lot."

His face fell. "No, I didn't mean…I mean—"

"I'm just giving you a hard time." Which she shouldn't do. He'd been amazing today.

"I'm sorry. I can't thank you enough. I'm sorry about your clothes."

His smile was tender. "You can throw up on me anytime, Ms. Harrison."

She groaned.

"I'm afraid your phone didn't survive."

His words pulled the unpleasant memory to the surface. "I'll get another one. I was thinking about an upgrade anyway."

He smiled. "Well, it isn't a new phone, but maybe this will cheer you up." He placed a small bag beside her on the bed. "I hope you won't get mad."

She peered into the bag. "You brought me clothes?"

"Yeah, I'm sorry if I upset you."

Poor guy was meeting himself coming and going.

"I was just trying—"

"I could kiss you!"

Jason's head flew up, his eyes meeting hers, his eyebrows arched in that quizzical look she remembered so well, his lips shockingly close to her own.

"I mean—"

He laughed. "I know what you mean."

Did he?

Did she?

A nurse bustled in, laptop in hand, to check vitals and O_2 sats. Jason stepped outside to give them some privacy and she was thankful for the interruption.

What was going on with her? He'd left. He didn't want to stay in North Carolina forever and she couldn't imagine living anywhere else. And while she understood his reasons, she had to admit she'd harbored the hope that maybe she would be enough of a reason to stay.

But she hadn't been.

Just because he was home now didn't mean he was home for good. He would be busy for the next several years helping care for his dad. When the inevitable came and duty wasn't tying him down anymore, would he bolt?

History said yes.

The nurse left and Jason returned. Henry

had dozed off by her side, and everyone had agreed to let him sleep.

"We need to talk."

"Okay." Could he tell how his presence messed with her?

"Your CO detectors didn't go off."

Oh. He wanted to talk about that. Of course he did. It was his job. So why had her heart sunk at his words?

"I noticed that."

"Your water heater was tampered with. The level of CO in the house was significantly higher than it should have been."

Her heart sank further. "Not an accident."

He shrugged. "If you hadn't caught the intruder, it would have looked like an accident. The tampering isn't obvious. Just a loose vent. The gas company guys apologized all over themselves. Said they couldn't understand how it happened."

"But they don't know about my visitor."

"Exactly."

"So what happens now? Can I go home? *Should* I go home?"

Jason couldn't meet her gaze.

"What aren't you telling me?"

He shifted from one foot to the other and shoved his hands in his pockets. "Don't get mad, but I called your brother."

"Great. He's probably already called Mom and Dad." Caroline exhaled. "I didn't want them to worry."

"Like they wouldn't want to know?"

She glared at him, hoping he could feel her displeasure burning from her retinas. "What did Blake say?"

"He tracked down Heidi."

"That didn't take long."

"I gather they have a system of some sort." He frowned at her. "Speaking of which, why did you call me?"

Heat flooded her cheeks. "I knew you were minutes away."

"Why not go to your front porch and yell at the officers sitting in your driveway?"

He wasn't going to let this go, was he? She didn't have a good answer.

"I wasn't thinking clearly," she said. "I was

afraid to leave Henry and I was afraid to get too far away from the bathroom."

He studied her longer than was comfortable, and she knew he hadn't fully accepted her response. Time to change the subject.

"So you spoke to Heidi?"

"Yeah. She said she'd call a friend. He's not far from here and he's going to come give your place a once-over. She doesn't want you to stay there until he's done."

Awesome. Heidi's definition of *once-over* probably meant pulling up the floors and tearing out the walls.

"I was able to convince her that we have things under control, but I won't be surprised if we wind up with some random FBI agents popping in and out."

Caroline blew out a breath. "I guess I should thank you again."

He winked, and her breath caught. "You may not be thanking me when you hear the rest of our plan."

"The plan?"

"I thought you could hang out with my mom

and dad while you're waiting for your house to be cleared."

Caroline fidgeted. "Are you sure that's a good idea? It looks like someone is trying to kill me. I should probably go to a deserted island, not hang out with your parents."

"Nonsense." Jason didn't seem as worried as he should be.

"I can't put your parents at risk. If anything happened to them—"

His hand on hers stopped her. "I've already talked to them. They understand what's going on, and they want you to come. Mom says she hasn't seen Henry in far too long."

"But—"

"Caroline. Dad's still a good shot."

She dropped her head in defeat. "I wasn't thinking that at all." Jason's dad had been a sniper. ALS would eventually rob him of the ability to hold a rifle, but at this point, he could probably outshoot 98 percent of the population.

"I know you weren't. He's been cleaning his rifle since I called. He's ready for anything.

And whoever is after you would have no reason to expect you to be there."

"Jason, I go to your parents' at least once a month."

"Heidi and I discussed that, but your visits are random and not something anyone would be able to use to target you."

"Are you sure?"

"Positive."

FIVE

At 1:00 p.m., Jason loaded Caroline and Henry into his car.

"Where'd you get the car seat?" Caroline strapped Henry in with practiced moves.

"Michael. He brought it from your house."

Caroline didn't respond. Had he upset her? "He was still there, so I asked him to grab it so we could get the little guy home." He pointed to a bag in the backseat. "He grabbed a bunch of clothes and diapers, too."

"That was very thoughtful." She laughed, a harsh sound with no humor in it. "To think that this time yesterday my biggest worry was if I'd allocated enough to the college fund I set up for this little guy." He saw the muscles in her jaw working overtime. "And now, I'm praying I can keep him alive until his second birthday." Her voice cracked on the last word, but when she looked up at him, no tears had broken free. She closed Henry's door. "You ready?"

"Almost."

He opened the passenger door for her. "There's one thing I've learned from combat." Her eyes filled with curiosity and concern. "You can't keep anyone alive."

She slumped in defeat and slid into the seat. He closed the door and leaned into the open window. "I'm not saying we don't do everything we can, but you have to let go of this feeling of accountability. You couldn't have kept Stephanie alive, and ultimately you can't keep Henry alive. Or yourself. Or me. Or anyone else you care about."

"Is this little speech supposed to be making me feel better? 'Cause it's not working."

He gripped the door. "It is supposed to help, actually. We can walk confidently into the next day, not because we've figured everything out and have thwarted the bad guys, but because we know the One who knows what they are up to. We walk confidently because we know He will help us."

Caroline looked away from him and spoke, so low he barely heard the words. "He didn't help Stephanie."

Ouch. *A little help here, Father?*

He walked around to the driver's seat and took his time buckling in. She continued to stare out the window as they pulled away from the curb.

"I lost friends in Afghanistan."

Her head whipped back to him. "I'm sorry."

The things this woman could make him do. He didn't talk about Afghanistan. Ever. But here he was talking about his darkest times. "When you head out on a patrol and you don't know if you'll be back for dinner, you have to dig deep to find the strength to follow orders and do your job. But when your friends don't make it home for dinner, you have to look outside of yourself to find any meaning in it."

Caroline sat ramrod straight beside him. He could barely tell if she was breathing.

"While God is Sovereign, we also live in a

fallen world. One where wars happen. Where evil men come after babies." He couldn't keep the disgust from his voice. "We have to trust He is working all things for ultimate good."

Even as he said the words, his mind flashed to his dad. The grim future he faced with grace, dignity and undaunted faith.

"I don't know why God allowed any of this. For Steph to fall in love with a guy who apparently got mixed up in some shady stuff. For her to get pregnant and leave the guy. For her to die. For her to leave you her baby. And now for someone to want either you or Henry, or both of you, out of the picture."

Caroline took an audible breath but didn't interrupt him as he continued.

"I do know He's not confused or surprised, and He will help us."

"I want to believe that," she said. "I really do."

He reached over, palm up. Would she take it?

She stared at his hand for a few moments, then laced her fingers through his. A long-dormant piece of his heart started throbbing. "I'll believe for both of us until you get there."

She squeezed his hand and turned to stare out the window. He assumed she didn't want him to see her face. Which was fine. He still had her hand in his, and he kept it until they pulled into his parents' driveway.

His mom was waiting for them, wearing a grin that stretched from one end of the front porch to the other. She bounded down the two steps and had Caroline wrapped in a bear hug before he could get around the car.

"Sweet girl, let's get you and your precious one inside. There's a bite in the air."

Caroline laughed. "Mama Drake, you would say there's a bite in the air if it was seventy degrees outside."

Caroline had Henry out of the car seat, and his mom grabbed him. "There's my handsome man. Henry, you've put on at least five pounds since you were here last. Let's get you some cookies so we can keep those numbers going!"

Jason trailed behind his mom and Caroline. His dad leaned against the porch rail, watching the procession. Their eyes met and he knew what his dad was thinking.

Could feel his mom's joy.

They'd always loved Caroline. Always dreamed of the day he'd bring her home as so much more than a friend.

Pretty sure they'd never imagined the time he'd bring her home along with her baby as the victims of a crime in need of protective custody.

But looking at the two of them—his mom cooing and his dad helping Henry give him a little fist bump—he wondered if they cared what the circumstances were.

She was here.

He was here.

For now.

Fifteen minutes later, Caroline left Henry in Mama Drake's capable hands and stepped onto the back deck. A tiny, screened room where at any time Mama Drake might have a pie cooling, a pitcher of tea that wouldn't fit in the fridge, or even a slow cooker bubbling with her famous mac and cheese.

Today, a pound cake tempted her from a pretty plate, and Caroline snagged a slice.

Jason had always been embarrassed about his home. Starting in middle school, he always wanted to go to her house instead of having her come to his. He'd started apologizing about the lack of channels on the TV or the lack of options in the kitchen.

Caroline wasn't so naive not to understand why. No, the Drakes weren't as well-off as her parents. But it hadn't mattered to her ever. The Drakes' home was always warm and welcoming, and while Caroline loved the sprawling home she'd grown up in, there was a coziness about the Drakes' tightly grouped rooms that couldn't be duplicated in five thousand square feet.

Jason hadn't seen it that way. He'd make little comments about money or status. If she dared to indicate that those things weren't important, he'd ask her how often she'd tried to live without them.

She'd refused to apologize for the life she'd been born into. They weren't wealthy by national standards, but they had more than most. Her parents had always stressed how fortunate they were compared with the majority of the people on the planet. She'd been trained to be thankful, and to feel a sense of responsibility to help those less fortunate.

But she'd never seen Jason as less fortunate. Their homes hadn't been similar in size, but they'd been similar in environment. He had two parents who loved him. Granted, there were plenty of problems with his birth father, but after his mom met Papa Drake, he'd always had a warm, clean home filled with light and laughter. A home she'd always been welcomed in. A place she'd never felt like she had to perform or pretend in. She didn't blame Jason for wanting more, but she wished he could see how much of what truly mattered was already here.

Caroline leaned against a porch support and closed her eyes. She had to pull it together. Had to find a way to make some sense of this mess. Someone wanted her dead. Why? How could she protect herself and her son?

"You okay?"

She turned at Jason's words and found him watching her through the open kitchen door.

"I didn't hear you."

"I know."

"How long have you been there?"

"Long enough to see you swipe my dessert."

She laughed. "There's plenty more."

He joined her in the small space. "What's on your mind?"

She stepped toward him and caught herself. What was she doing? This was a bad idea. She could not let herself get emotionally entangled. Not with anyone, but especially not with Jason Drake. She'd gone down that path.

She knew how it ended.

She knew how much it hurt.

Caroline rocked back on her heels. "Just trying to figure out what's going on."

Jason stared out over the backyard. "Me, too. I need to head out for a little while."

"You've been with me all day. I'm sure you

have other responsibilities, other cases you need to be working on. Go. You don't have to babysit—"

"I'm not babysitting you." His face darkened. "I'm doing my job. You're a citizen of this community, which I have sworn to protect, and someone is trying to kill you. It is, in fact, my job to be sure that doesn't happen."

He was right, of course. She tried to keep her expression neutral. "I understand, and I appreciate that."

He stepped closer, and when she tried to back up, she slammed into a porch column. "Ow." She rubbed the back of her head.

Jason didn't back up or give her the space she'd been seeking. "Are you okay?"

She nodded, avoiding eye contact. But he didn't allow that, cupping his hand under her chin and tilting it up until their eyes met.

"It's my job to protect you, but it's also my privilege. I'd be doing it whether I had the badge to make it official or not." His eyes flashed with intensity as he spoke. "I need to check on a few things and run by the office to get some files that might help us figure out what's going on."

"Okay." She didn't trust herself to try to say anything else.

"Try not to worry. Mom's thrilled you're here. Dad's on alert. There are uniformed officers patrolling the perimeter of the property. I'll be back before you know it."

He stared into her eyes longer than she wanted him to. Her heartbeat pulsed in her ears. One of his eyebrows ticked up, and she had to wonder if in the silence of the porch, he could hear it.

She needed to get a grip. This wasn't high school. He wasn't the best friend she wanted to be more. Given their history, she'd trust him to protect every part of her.

Except her heart.

He stepped back, breaking the moment. He winked and turned back to the house.

She heard him speak to his mom, then his dad.

Then... Henry?

Jason's fondness for Henry was a surprise.

He'd never been a big fan of kids, and he'd always said he'd never have any of his own. Said he wouldn't risk being the kind of father his own birth father was.

She doubted that had changed.

He was being kind to Henry because he was a kind man, but that didn't mean he wanted children. Just like he didn't want to live in North Carolina.

She'd built her whole life around her home, her family, her community—and now, her son. She couldn't let herself forget that it was the kind of life Jason didn't want. Then, now or ever.

SIX

Jason walked around Caroline's house. Again. This was his third pass. Each time he moved out another fifty feet. Michael joined him.

"What are we doing?" Michael asked.

"Looking."

"Fine," Michael said. "Let's talk about the case while we walk."

"Okay," Jason said. "Start with Caroline's work."

Michael pulled out a small notebook. "She's changed a few suppliers, like she said, but no one I've spoken to at the plant believes any of them would be angry enough to come after her. Blake agreed with that assessment when you talked to him?"

Jason nodded. "He did. He insists everything is business as usual at HPI. He said

Caroline drives a hard bargain and is a great negotiator. Part of her job is to keep their expenses down, and she takes that seriously, but she treats everyone fairly and the business community respects her for it." He stopped and looked back at the house, trying to see what an intruder would see from here. "She claims she doesn't have a boyfriend and hasn't had one in a while."

"Not for lack of trying," Michael said under his breath.

"What?"

Michael's grin had a taunting edge to it. "She's the most eligible bachelorette in the county. She's gorgeous, smart and rich."

Was Michael trying to push his buttons?

"Of course," Michael went on, "she's also funny, kind, has a great personality, and—"

"I get it, Michael." Jason returned to walking. "She's a catch."

Michael smirked. "People assume she is, of course, but given that no one has caught her since college, she's more like an urban myth."

"What is that supposed to mean?"

Michael grabbed a branch and pushed it out of his way. "You know exactly what it means. If you don't, you're an idiot."

How much could Michael possibly know about his past with Caroline? He'd been a grade behind them in school. They'd been friends, played sports together, but he had never confided anything about his feelings for Caroline to anybody.

Jason tried to keep his tone neutral when he replied. "I'm afraid I have no idea what you're talking about, nor do I see how any of this relates to the case."

Michael laughed. "I know a dozen guys who've tried to get close enough to ask her out. I know only five who succeeded in asking her, and she turned them all down."

"Your point?"

"You've made more progress in twenty-four hours than anyone has. Ever. Makes a guy wonder."

Michael was like the annoying little brother who wouldn't stop pestering you until he'd made you mad. "The only progress I've made is on this case, and it isn't much progress at all."

That wiped the teasing look off Michael's face. "I disagree that there's no progress. The problem isn't that we don't have anything to go on, it's that we don't like where it's taking us."

Jason stopped under a pine. From here, he had a decent angle on one of the windows. Could the intruder have watched Caroline from here? The thought made his blood boil. There were a few broken branches, a piece of trash—

He knelt beside the paper. Up close it looked more like a photograph. He pulled a glove from his pocket and used it to pick up the faded page. He tried to keep his voice calm. "What can you tell me about Henry?"

"Not much. I worked the car accident when Steph died. It was…" Michael shook his head like he wanted to shake away the memories. "We went over that car thoroughly. Heidi helped. That was before she and Blake married." He laughed, but there was no humor in it. "Heidi is great, but she has a tendency to assume the worst. She tried to hide it from Caroline, but she was concerned about foul play."

"Was there any?"

"Not that we could find. It was one of those senseless tragedies you hear about on the news. 'Mother of young child fatally injured in car wreck on I-26.' We see it all the time, but I never get used to it."

Which was one of the reasons he'd always liked Michael. The guy could be annoying, but he had a soft heart. "I'm not saying you're wrong, but we're going to have to review that case again," Jason said as he flipped the paper in his hand over. There was no mistaking it. The photo was of Caroline and Henry. Both of their faces were circled. He handed it to Michael.

Michael's eyes widened.

"Caroline doesn't have any enemies, and the only skeleton in Stephanie's closet was her husband. Whatever reason someone has for targeting them has got to do with that man. And that means we need to figure out who the father is. Discreetly. I'll talk to Caroline about it again tonight. Pick her brain for any details Stephanie might have let slip." He glanced back at the house. "We won't be able to do much over the weekend, but we need to get a fresh set of eyes on Stephanie's accident, just to be sure. All the county offices will be closed, but let's shoot for having a list of places to call by Monday morning."

Someone had already tried to kill Caroline and Henry twice in the past twenty-four hours. Was there any chance they could make it through the weekend without someone trying again?

He and Michael returned to the station and spent the next three hours going over everything on Stephanie's accident. He couldn't find any fault with the investigation or the conclusions.

"Let's get out of here," Jason finally said. "Want to come to the house? With Caroline there, I'm sure Mom has outdone herself for dinner."

Michael raised his hand. "Sorry, man, I'm

picking Cathy up around eight. But call me if you need me."

"I will."

Jason's phone rang as he walked through the parking lot. He took one look at the number and declined the call. He slid into the seat of his Explorer, anxiety scratching its way through his mind.

He'd been back in town six months. This was the first night he'd been in a hurry to get home.

Caroline had a new appreciation for the way the tigers at the zoo must feel. She'd tried to sit but couldn't keep from fidgeting, so she'd switched to helping Mama Drake in the kitchen.

Henry was having a grand time playing with a huge pot and a wooden spoon, but his joyful cacophony couldn't drown out the terror pulsing in her heart. She stirred the green beans and kept up a light banter with Mama Drake, but even the lush aroma of pot roast

and made-from-scratch biscuits couldn't set-
tle her nerves.

Jason would be home soon. He wouldn't let
anything happen to her or Henry. She knew
that. Well, she knew he would try to keep
them safe. Maybe even die trying. What if
someone came after her here? What if everybody she loved wound up dead?

All because of her. The thought nauseated
her.

Papa Drake had smiled and welcomed her
in, but she could sense a level of alertness per-
meating the air that she'd never experienced
in this house. Jason's home had always been
safe. Fun. Light.

She'd brought the heavy darkness. She
should take Henry and leave, but where could
she go?

The screen door clanged and Caroline's
hand jerked so hard she slopped bean juice
over the side of the pan. A second later her
mind overruled her nerves as she processed
the voices in the other room. Jason was home.

She hurried to grab a towel to clean up the mess before she set the burner smoking.

"There you are," Mama Drake called out as Jason entered the small kitchen. "Just in time. Biscuits will be out of the oven in three minutes. You have time to wash up."

He pecked his mom's cheek. "Yes, ma'am." He threw a wink in Caroline's direction before heading down the short hallway.

Caroline couldn't tell if he'd learned anything or not, and she knew he wouldn't say much at dinner. Part of her wanted answers now. Part of her didn't want to add any more stress to the Drakes' home. Part of her wanted to run.

A big part of her.

If it wasn't for Henry, she might do it. Just get in her car and take off. Except she didn't currently have a car. And even if she did, how did anyone run with a baby? How could she protect him?

A prayer bubbled in her spirit. *Father, please help us. Show me what to do. Show me how to get us out of this mess.*

It had been a while since she'd prayed this way. Would God even listen?

Even as she asked the question, she already knew the answer. He would hear her.

As Jason returned to the kitchen, her fear abated, but her emotions took off on a whole new tangent. He stepped behind her, his free hand resting on her waist for a second as he sampled the mashed potatoes Mama Drake had whipped to perfection.

She tried to ignore the way her body responded to his casual touch. It would have been easier if she wasn't trying to keep her breathing steady.

"Did you make these?" He grinned at her. He clearly hadn't forgotten some of her more impressive kitchen disasters.

"I did not, but I'll have you know that my cooking skills have improved dramatically since high school."

"Really." His dry tone didn't disguise his skepticism. "I might need proof."

"Fine. Dinner. I choose the menu. You eat the food. No matter what."

"It's a date." He spoke the words with a laugh, but the lighthearted moment faded as his eyes held hers.

Had she lost her mind? Had she asked Jason Drake on a date? No, she hadn't. But she had invited him to dinner and *he* had announced it was a date. Why?

She hoped he couldn't read the turmoil in her eyes.

Mama Drake bustled in. "Jason, honey, grab those biscuits from the oven, won't you?"

Caroline turned back to the beans. Maybe he would assume the flush on her cheeks came from the heat of the stove.

Not likely.

Caroline had no idea how she survived dinner. The food, delicious as always, stuck in her throat. She didn't want to be rude to Mama Drake, but it was requiring all the energy she had to make small talk.

What if someone was outside the house right now? She hadn't missed Jason's all-too-casual way of closing the blinds and pulling the curtains in the small dining room. Was he worried, too?

She looked up from her plate and found his eyes on her. One quirked eyebrow from him and she knew. She might be making a decent show for the Drakes, but Jason wasn't fooled. He could still read her, and he knew how scared she was.

When the dishes were done, the Drakes retired to their room. She could hear them talking, heard the TV announce the beginning of a two-hour special for a reality show, heard Papa Drake laugh low. The sound seemed alien to her with the weight of so much death and dying and loss wrapped around her. Bowed down under it, she sank into the sofa, Henry asleep on her shoulder.

Jason joined her and told her about the photo he'd found at her house.

"What happens now?" She kept her voice down. "I can't stay here, Jason, but where do I go?"

"You most certainly can stay here. For tonight at least. Hopefully those FBI agents your sister-in-law is sending will check everything out and you'll be able to go home tomorrow."

"That doesn't fix anything. Someone is trying to kill us and we have no idea why." Jason didn't argue with her. "What did you go to the office for this afternoon?"

"I wanted to look through everything we had on Stephanie's accident."

"Find anything?"

"Nope. Just a tragic accident. Senseless and without a scrap of evidence of foul play."

"I could have told you that."

Jason smiled. "I needed to see it for myself. Sometimes a fresh set of eyes can pick up on something others missed."

"So is this about me or Henry?"

"I don't know. I'm not ruling out the possibility that you are the primary target, but so far I can't find any motive for killing you because of your own actions or relationships. Blake insists there's no drama at the plant. No one can find any threat against your family. I'm going back through the files we have on the attack at the plant last year to see if maybe you're being targeted by the same people, but the general theory is that if they wanted to take you out, they wouldn't have bothered with carbon monoxide. And that if they had sent someone to shoot you, he would have finished the job before running off. No way he would have been scared off by the sirens."

He propped his feet on the coffee table. "Heidi's work has been almost exclusively undercover, but she's doing some checking to see if any of her enemies might be out to get to her through you. But it seems unlikely. Whatever this is about, it seems more likely that it's tied to Henry."

Caroline rested her head on Henry's soft hair. "I can't think of anyone who would want to kill me, and I have no idea why they would want to harm Henry. He's no threat to any-one. We don't even know who his dad is, and honestly, I don't care."

"I think you may need to start caring."

She had no reply to that, so for a moment they sat without speaking, the sound from the TV in his parents' room the only noise. She heard singing and cheering, and then a commercial break, before he spoke.

"If someone is trying to kill Henry, then the birth father is the only lead we have. Stephanie's been dead almost a year. Her family has no wealth or connections. She has no siblings, and there's no reason we can find that anyone affiliated with her would have any reason to harm Henry. That leaves us with the father. We have to find him. Get DNA. Confirm he's dead. Find out who he knew. Who his family is. I'm not going to lie to you—I have no idea how we're going to figure it out. But we have to try."

"He's dead. Steph said—"

"Do you have a name? A death certificate? An arrest record? Anything to corroborate what she told you?"

Caroline could taste bile as her body reacted faster than her mind. She forced herself to swallow. "You think she lied to me? To her parents?"

"I'm not saying that," Jason said. "She might have told you what she believed to be true, but we don't know where she was getting her information. So we need to find out. Even if everything she told you was true, there's still the question of what he did to wind up in jail and what he did to wind up dead."

"But whatever he did, why would that cause people to come after us?" Henry started at her outburst, and she patted his back and took a deep breath as he resettled, his little mouth falling open in sleep. "It's not like Henry's a threat. He's just a baby."

"I agree he's just a baby, but I can't agree he's not a threat."

How could Henry be a threat to anyone? "I don't understand."

"Caroline," Jason said. "There are people out there who kill for no apparent reason, but they are the exception."

She could hear it in his tone, the way he was trying to explain without angering her. Or terrifying her. Or both.

"In almost every case, there's a motive. And given that Henry is young, never knew his father, barely knew his mother and will have no true memories of either of them, then that leaves us with only one possibility."

"What?"

"That Henry is a threat simply by being alive. Not because of what he knows or remembers, but because of who he is. And if that's the case, then we have to find out who he is."

Caroline shook her head. "I can't believe this is happening. Not now. Not when I'm so close to finalizing everything. I haven't cared one bit about finding Henry's father's family because it was the one thing that was clear in Stephanie's will. The birth father's family was to have nothing to do with him. Ever. Which makes me feel certain that Steph was protecting Henry from them."

"Stephanie left you a message in the will?"

"It's not really a will. It's a trust document. More private than a will. It said that it was her request that Henry never know his father's family. I've tried to honor her request."

Jason's face paled. "Caroline, please tell me

all the adoption proceedings have included looking into the situation with the father."

"Of course they have." She heard the frustration in her tone. "We've done everything we were supposed to do. The courts have put out notices looking for him. But with no name to go on, his parental rights were revoked in absentia. It's not that uncommon." She did not like the way Jason was looking at her. "Jason?"

He shook his head. "Something about this doesn't make sense. Either he is not dead and is coming after his own child, or he *is* dead and someone else wants to be sure no part of him lives on."

He put a hand on Henry's back. "Either way, it certainly looks like this little guy is in grave danger."

SEVEN

Jason sat straight up and tried to focus on what had wakened him. Sleep fled as he heard footsteps in the hall, moving toward where he'd made a bed for himself on the living room couch. His chest tightened as he slid his hand toward his weapon.

"Don't shoot, son." He relaxed as his dad's soft voice floated toward him in the darkness.

"What are you doing, Dad?"

"Thought I heard something outside."

Was that what had woken him up? Could someone be in the yard?

"What did it sound like?" Jason asked.

His dad sat beside him on the sofa but kept the rifle he'd brought with him from the bedroom. "Not sure. Something that didn't belong in the night. I didn't want to turn on a bunch of lights and scare the ladies, so I thought I'd put you on alert. Of course, you already were."

Jason's heart warmed at the pride in his father's voice. "What are you thinking?"

"I'd say call your buddies and have them scope things out. And I think you should peek in on Caroline and Henry. Make sure they're okay. Then maybe we should stay up for a while. Morning's not too far off."

Morning was a solid three hours away, but he had to hand it to his dad. The man did what needed to be done. Always had.

He checked in with the officers on patrol outside. They were fine and hadn't seen anything suspicious, but they had been on the far side of the property and were just now headed back toward the house. He eased from the sofa and crept down the hall, then paused at the door to his room. He hated to invade Caroline's privacy, and he also hated to wake her. She needed to rest.

He rested one hand on the doorknob and

turned it a millimeter at a time. He eased the door open.

"Take one more step and it will be the last thing you do," Caroline's voice hissed from the darkness. His eyes could just make out her form, sitting on the bed, weapon aimed straight at him.

"Caroline, it's me," he whispered.

"Jason!" She jumped from the bed and came straight at him. He opened his arms, expecting her to need comfort. She slugged his shoulder.

"Don't ever do that to me again!" He'd never known it was possible for someone to whisper and yell at the same time. "I could have shot you!"

"I wasn't expecting to find you sitting there pointing a weapon at the door. Please tell me you haven't been sitting like that all night?"

"Of course not." She punched him again. A little bit gentler, but not much.

"Would you quit hitting me?"

"Would you explain why you're creeping into my room?"

"Technically, it's my room, but if you must know, I was checking on you."

"Why?"

He didn't want to tell her, but she had a right to know. "Dad and I both thought we heard something outside. Probably a deer or raccoon, but it woke us both. I wanted to make sure you and Henry were okay."

She slumped against the wall. "I thought I heard something, too," she said.

"Dad and I are both up and armed. The officers patrolling haven't seen anything, but I'm going to go check it out, so when you hear some noise, don't worry. Why don't you lie back down?"

"Like I could sleep now."

"Fine. I'll be back with a report in a few minutes."

"Be careful."

Her concern warmed his heart as he slid out the back door and paused in the darkness. He gave his eyes time to adjust to the dark. He didn't want to turn on the flashlight and make himself a target until he had some backup.

His dad was sitting in the hall. No one would get past him. But had someone been outside? And were they still here?

Tires on the driveway alerted him to the arrival of the additional officers he'd requested to take a look around. He eased around the back of the house and met them at the front porch.

"There are no obvious signs of anyone near the house," he told them. "Let's take a look around, see if anything is out of the ordinary."

They scoured the area surrounding the house but didn't see anything suspicious. The cars didn't appear to have been tampered with, and there were no obvious footprints or tire tracks in places they didn't belong.

If someone had been out there, they'd had the good sense to leave.

He thanked the officers and reentered the house.

"All clear," he told his dad.

The only reply he received was a grunt. It didn't matter what they didn't find. His dad wasn't going to sleep tonight.

Caroline popped her head out of the bedroom door. "Find anything?"

"No." He walked over to her. "Try to get some sleep. Henry has no idea what's going on, and he's going to need you tomorrow. Leave the bedroom door open. One of us will stay in the hallway. You'll be safe."

No one was coming in this house tonight. Not if they wanted to live to tell about it.

Caroline blew out a long breath. "I'm so sorry to have brought this on you. On your parents. Your dad should be resting, not sitting up all night with a gun."

"He's fine," he assured her. "I think if it wasn't for the fact that this is all deadly serious, he'd be enjoying himself."

"Men."

He almost smiled, but his mind was on what could have been outside—and why. "Exactly. So go back to sleep. We'll be right here."

"Fine."

She crawled back into the bed and placed the gun on the nightstand.

"Caroline?"

"What?"

"Don't take this the wrong way, but do you know how to use that thing?"

She laughed again. "Heidi made it her mission to turn all of us into gun-safety experts. I'm a really good shot."

He was looking forward to meeting this Heidi.

"I hope you never have to aim it at a person, but it's good to know you can. Now go to sleep."

"Yes, sir." It was hard to tell in the dark, but it looked like she threw him a little salute before she rolled over on her side.

He slid back into the hall and found his dad standing at the end of it. "Everything okay, Dad?"

"Yeah. Glad she didn't shoot you earlier."

"Me, too."

"She's a tough one. Doesn't look like it on the outside, but she's made of strong stock."

"She is."

"When you gonna get over yourself and marry her?"

"Dad!"

His dad chuckled. "I'm gonna sit over in the kitchen. You take the hall. We'll switch in an hour. Tap the floor twice if you need me."

"Yes, sir."

Jason stood in the hall. Caroline's soft breathing sounded steady and slow. He could hear his mom snoring. His ears strained for any sounds that didn't belong as he settled in for a watchful night.

Henry's cry pierced the air. Caroline was on her feet by the pack 'n' play before she even registered that she was awake.

"Shh." She scooped him up and carried him back to her bed.

"Mama." Henry patted her arm. "Mama," he said again. She took a deep breath, inhaling the familiar scent of baby shampoo.

Henry tolerated the cuddling for less than a minute. He squirmed his way to the edge and slid his feet over first. As soon as they hit the ground, he took off for the door. Caroline threw the covers back and followed him.

She didn't want to think about what her hair looked like, but at least she'd had the good sense to sleep in her clothes last night.

She dashed down the hall in time to see Jason scooping Henry into a bear hug. "Whoa, little man. Where do you think you're going?" He smiled at Henry as he spoke, but she could hear the fatigue in his voice. See it on his features. She followed behind as Jason carried Henry into the kitchen.

"I think you need some breakfast. Mama Drake has French toast and bacon almost ready. You like French toast, don't you?"

"Of course he does," Mama Drake said. "Who doesn't love French toast?" She spotted Caroline. "Good morning, dear. Did you get enough sleep? Do you want to go rest some more? We can handle Henry."

"Thank you, but I think I should freshen Henry up a little bit before he eats."

Even though she'd avoided using the words *diaper change*, Jason's expression was the funniest thing Caroline had seen in days. He held Henry toward her like he was a bundle of toxic waste. "Here ya go."

Mama Drake's laughter and Papa Drake's teasing followed her down the hall. She changed Henry's diaper, put him in a clean outfit and ran a comb through his hair. Blond, curly hair that was nothing like Stephanie's. She had to admit, the curls were precious.

She examined Henry as she slid on his socks. She could see Stephanie in him every now and then, but she suspected this child bore a strong resemblance to his father.

She tried to think about anything Stephanie had ever told her about Henry's father. Caroline had thought about him plenty of times, but she had to admit never with an ounce of compassion. When she thought of him, it was always with disgust and disdain.

Stephanie had loved him—so whatever he had done that made her leave, it had to be horrible. And then, assuming Stephanie hadn't been lying to her, he'd landed in jail and gotten himself killed.

Was it possible his sins were reaching past the grave and into Henry's future?

A light tap on the door broke her from her musing.

"Caroline? Everything okay? Mom says breakfast is ready."

"I'm coming."

Jason stepped into the room, eyes narrowed in concern. "What's wrong?"

She tried to shake it off. "Just thinking about what you said. Wishing Steph had been more open. She trusted me with her son, I wish she'd trusted me with more about his father."

Jason rubbed his hand over the stubble on his chin. "Well, since you've brought it up…"

"Brought what up?"

"Stephanie."

"What about her?"

"Do you think you'd be up for paying her parents a visit?"

Caroline knew where this was headed. "You think they might know something I don't?"

"Maybe. Or they might know something that they don't realize they know."

Could they do this? Could they put her friend's parents through this pain again? She looked at Henry. Yes. They could. They had to.

"It will be hard. They don't like to talk about Stephanie at all. After her death, Mrs. Crawford sank into a deep depression, and honestly, Mr. Crawford wasn't much better. They've struggled to make sense of it." Hadn't they all? But she had Henry, and he kept her too busy to grieve. Well, to grieve much. "But you're right. I'll call them after breakfast. Maybe we can run over there this afternoon. What day is it, anyway?"

Jason groaned. "It's Saturday."

"Really?"

Jason nodded. "Feels like it's been about a year, but it's only been a little over thirty-six hours."

Thirty-six hours? She looked at Jason. How was it possible that the past thirty-six hours had erased the past thirteen years of distance between them? It already felt like he'd never left. Like she could trust him.

He held her eyes. Could he sense how confusing this was for her? Did he have any idea how many questions she wanted to ask him and how afraid she was of his answers?

"Let's eat," he said, deliberately ignoring the tension between them. "Let's figure out what's going on with Henry." He turned to the door, then paused. "But when this is over, you and I need to finish our talk."

Indeed.

Breakfast was as lighthearted as she could have hoped for under the circumstances. Mama and Papa Drake kept up an easy banter. Henry provided solid entertainment by licking syrup off his plate, spilling his milk and running sticky hands through his curls.

Mama Drake volunteered for bath duty and whisked Henry down the hall, giving Caroline an opportunity to call Stephanie's parents.

Part of her hoped they wouldn't be home, but Stephanie's mom answered on the second ring.

"Hello?"

"Mrs. Crawford."

"Caroline? How is everything?"

She swallowed hard. "Not great, Mrs. Crawford, I'm afraid."

"Is everyone okay? Is Henry—"

"He's fine, but we've had a couple of situations over the past few days that have left us with some concerns. I was wondering if I could come over and talk to you. About Stephanie."

The silence on the other end of the line lasted long enough that Caroline worried Mrs. Crawford might have dropped the phone.

"Mrs. Crawford?"

A sharp intake of breath came through the line. "Of course, dear. Whatever you need."

"Thank you." Now for the fun part. "I'm going to have someone with me. Do you remember Jason Drake?"

"Yes. I heard he'd come back home."

"Yes, ma'am. He's a police officer now. A detective."

"I don't know how much help we can be to a detective, but of course we'll talk to him. You're bringing my grandson?"

"Yes, ma'am. Definitely."

"Okay. When should we look for you?"

"Would eleven be okay?"

"Of course, dear. We'll see you then."

When Caroline returned to the living room, Papa Drake was perched on the edge of the sofa, which wouldn't have been particularly unusual if it hadn't been for the rifle he cradled in his left arm. He certainly hadn't had that with him at the breakfast table. What had made him pull it out again?

"What's going on?" she asked.

Papa Drake patted the sofa. "Nothing to fret over."

"Then why are you sitting here with a rifle?"

"I like rifles." He winked at her.

"I know that, sir, but I've been coming to this house since I was in elementary school and I've never seen you sit on the sofa with one."

He grinned. "New habit."

"Because of me." How could he joke about this?

He faced her, no trace of amusement left

in his expression. "Young lady, you can get that out of your head right now. None of this is because of you. Someone is so lost they've reached a place where ending another life seems to be the only solution. That's a sin problem right there. Not a Caroline Harrison problem. Not a Henry problem. Not even a Stephanie problem." He patted the rifle. "I've lived a long time without needing to face problems this way. I'd prefer not to need to do it again, but if someone chooses to attempt to harm anyone in my home, I won't sit by and allow it to happen." He smiled at her. "Jason's out walking the property. Looking for any signs of the cause of last night's racket. I'm just taking a few extra precautions while he's out."

A hand gripped her heart. Jason was out there, where their attacker might be.

The sound of footsteps on the porch made her jump. "It's me," Jason said before he'd even come into view. He stepped inside. "I couldn't find anything. Not that I'm a skilled tracker, but all I saw were the usual critters."

Caroline blew out a breath in relief, but she didn't miss the look of concern that passed between father and son. Just because he hadn't found anything didn't mean no one had been out there.

A danger she couldn't see stalked her.

When would they strike next?

EIGHT

Jason held the door for Caroline as she maneuvered through it with the diaper bag on one arm and Henry's hand held tightly in hers.

"Come on, buddy. Let's go see your grandma and grandpa!"

Henry said something that did not sound like grandma or grandpa, but maybe it was supposed to because Caroline said, "Yes, that's right. Grandma and Grandpa."

Once they were down the stairs, Jason ran to the car and opened the passenger door. "Here," he said. "Let me." He picked Henry up.

He placed him into the car seat and fiddled with the straps. He heard Caroline's laughter behind him. "Let me. We're running late. I'll show you how it works later."

He stepped back and watched as she buckled Henry in before climbing in herself. Henry started to fuss before they'd made it to the end of the driveway. Caroline reached inside the diaper bag at her feet and grabbed a book.

"Ow!" She slapped her arm.

"You okay?"

"Something stung me," she said. She examined the dead bug. "A fire ant. That's weird."

Henry's fussing changed. Before he'd sounded aggravated. Now? Mad. Or maybe hurt.

"It's okay, baby," Caroline said. "You love this one." She turned toward the backseat with the book in her hand.

And screamed.

"No! Stop! Stop!" She fumbled with her seat belt as he slammed on the brakes.

"What is it?" He threw the Explorer into Park and turned to see what had Caroline in such a panic.

Henry sat strapped into his car seat, tears trickling down his face, as at least thirty ants crawled over his arms and legs. He squirmed to get away, but he was held fast by the car seat straps.

Caroline jumped from the Explorer and rushed to his side of the car. Jason beat her to it. Thankfully he'd been paying attention earlier. It took only a few seconds to free Henry from the seat. Seconds that felt like hours as Henry's wails sliced through the air.

As soon as he pulled the boy from the restraints, Jason set Henry on the ground. "Get his shoes off," he said to Caroline as he pulled off Henry's long-sleeved shirt. Red welts had already exploded all over his little torso.

Jason ignored the stings to his fingers and hands. He had to get the nasty creatures off Henry.

Caroline moved fast. She had Henry's shoes and socks off and was pulling his pants off when Jason heard the screen door slam and his mother's worried cry. In his peripheral vision he noted the rifle in his dad's hands and the way he wasn't watching them but was scanning the surrounding area.

"Mom, go run a bath. A cool one. Quick! Throw some oatmeal in it. Or baking soda."

The screen door slamming again was the only indication he had that she'd heard him.

Caroline got Henry stripped down, and they brushed every fire ant they could see off his tiny body.

"See any more?"

Caroline ran her fingers through Henry's hair. "I don't think so. Let's get him in the tub so we can drown anything that's still hiding."

He wanted to follow her, but right now he could be more help if he stayed put. With Caroline inside, he turned to his dad. "Do you mind keeping an eye out while I check the car?"

He got a quick nod in response.

Jason turned to the Explorer. Henry's car seat had been in there since he'd brought them home from the hospital yesterday. The Explorer had been locked, and he'd noticed no signs of tampering when he'd looked around this morning.

He studied the car seat without touching it. Fire ants swarmed all over it.

No way this was an accident.

What kind of monster would do this to a kid?

Ants now swarmed all over the driver's seat. A quick glance at the passenger seat indicated the same. If Henry hadn't reacted as quickly as he did, they would have been driving down the road when the ants started stinging both him and Caroline. He could have easily wrecked and they all could have been killed.

Jason pulled his phone from his pocket and brushed a fire ant off it before dialing Michael's number.

"What's up?"

"I need a crime scene team out to my parents' house."

"What?"

Jason explained what had happened.

Michael responded by saying all the things Jason wished he could say. When he'd calmed down, he assured Jason they'd be out there in a few minutes and he'd find an exterminator while he was at it.

Jason pocketed his phone. *Father, what on earth is going on?*

Caroline smacked at another fire ant.

Man, those little monsters hurt! She looked at Henry floating in the tub. Mama Drake had gone into full home-remedy mode. The scent of oatmeal and apple cider vinegar permeated the tiny bathroom.

"How many bites did he get?" Caroline asked.

"I count twelve. Mostly on his arms and chest. I didn't see any abnormal swelling and he's breathing fine, so it looks like you don't have to worry about him having too severe of a reaction. Might not hurt to give him a little bit of an antihistamine, though."

Caroline leaned against the door. "That's a good idea. I have plenty at home."

But was home safe? Even to run inside and grab an over-the-counter medication? She closed her eyes and blew out a breath.

"Don't you worry about it, sweet girl. I'll take care of it."

Mama Drake disappeared down the hall, and Caroline took her spot on the closed toilet. Her phone buzzed. A text from her brother checking on her. She stared at the phone. What could she say? *Oh, we're fine. Someone is trying to kill us all, but other than that...*

As much as she missed her brother's wisdom and insight, she was relieved that he'd been away for the past few days. Having him and her niece, Maggie, home meant having them in harm's way. Not that they hadn't been there before, but this was getting ridiculous.

She tried to think of how to frame her answer to Blake. She typed in three different versions and deleted them all. A tap on the door startled her.

"Everything okay?" Jason asked.

She waved her phone. "Blake wants an update."

"I'm sure he's worried."

"I'm sure he'll be more worried after I tell him about this."

A sound from the living room pulled Jason's attention away. "I'll be right back."

He returned with a bottle of medication and a small spoon.

"Where did that come from?"

"Mom told me what you needed and suggested we call Michael. He picked it up at the Triangle Stop on his way over with the crime scene team."

He handed her the bottle, his face a mask of worry. "Should we get Henry checked out by the pediatrician? He got a lot of bites."

Jason going paternal again?

"This is one time I'm thankful he doesn't have my highly allergic genes," she said. "He's breathing fine. There's no major swelling. We'll keep an eye on him, but I think he's fine."

"You're the expert," he said. "Speaking of, how are you?"

Caroline smiled. "My EpiPen is in my pocket, but I only got a couple of bites. Nothing to worry about." Jason shook his head, and she thought about what she'd said. "Okay, plenty to worry about, but I've never needed to use an EpiPen for anything other than peanut exposure, and today's incident hasn't changed that."

"I called the Crawfords," he said.

"What did you tell them?"

"That something had come up. I asked if we could come later this afternoon. They were fine with that."

"Do you think we should go over there?"

Jason seemed surprised by her question. "I thought we'd agreed we need to talk to them."

"We do, but what if we bring our bad guys with us?"

Jason shook his head. "I don't think that's going to be an issue. No one's tried to harm my parents. Putting the ants in the car shows they're still targeting Henry and you."

"It doesn't seem like they tried too hard with this one. How stupid do you have to be to try to kill someone with fire ants?"

"You're either stupid or very smart. It's impossible to trace. We found little canisters— one in Henry's seat, one in the passenger seat, one in the driver's seat. When we sat down, it allowed the ants to crawl out."

"Yeah, but fire ants?"

"Well, you can be sure a fire ant will bite whatever it comes into contact with. And Henry's small. Little kids have been killed from fire ant bites, especially when there are several in a row."

Caroline poured the pink medicine into the spoon. Did Jason notice how her hand shook?

"Someone broke into the Explorer last night—did it without leaving a trace—and planted the fire ants. Maybe they hoped we'd run off the road in the confusion? I don't know what the reasoning was."

She spooned the medicine into Henry's mouth. He drank it without complaint. She stared at his face. The red welts on his arms screamed at her that she wasn't enough to protect this precious child. Why was this happening? "Nowhere is safe, is it?"

Jason's face confirmed her worst fears. "Right now, the best solution is to find out who is behind this. Once we know who they are and understand what they're up to, we'll be able to fight back."

Fighting back seemed like a great idea right now.

"Let's have some lunch and go see the Crawfords," he said.

Jason's phone buzzed. He glanced at it, then back to Caroline. "It's your sister-in-law. She wants me to give her regular updates, and she says someone is at your house right now reviewing the security system. You may be able to go home tonight."

Home. Her own room. Her own bed. It sounded lovely, but would they be safe?

"We need to tell them to check for fire ants."

He smiled. "Already done. Come on. Mom's love language is food. She's made sandwiches, and she won't be happy until we eat."

"Go ahead. I'll be there in a few minutes."

"Need any help with Henry?" he asked.

Again with the paternal stuff? "No. I'm good. Thanks."

Jason left. She dried Henry and dressed

him in clean clothes that she'd inspected thoroughly. She pulled him into her arms.

Father, help us. Show us. Give us something to go on. Protect us. Protect Henry. Protect Jason.

Three sandwiches, yet another change of clothes for Henry thanks to a leaky sippy cup, a car seat borrowed from a neighbor and two hours later, Caroline knocked on the Crawfords' door.

"Come in, come in!" Mrs. Crawford opened the door with a warm smile, her eyes roving over Henry. "There's my sweet man. Come in!"

They stepped into the entryway of the split-level house. Mrs. Crawford led the way up the stairs, and they settled in the den. They visited for a few minutes, Mr. Crawford bouncing Henry on his knee until Henry wanted to get down to explore the room. Mrs. Crawford gladly followed him around, but when he toppled into a coffee table and spilled a glass of tea, Caroline scooped him into her lap and gave Jason a look that he correctly interpreted.

"Mr. and Mrs. Crawford," Jason said. "I'm sorry to bring up a difficult subject, but we need to talk to you about Stephanie."

Silence.

The room pressed in around her. Henry squirmed in her arms. The Crawfords stared at the floor. She had time to dig through the diaper bag and find two toy trains to distract Henry before Jason cleared his throat.

"Stephanie was my friend," he said. Mrs. Crawford's eyes flew to Jason's face. "Many of my fondest memories of childhood include her, and I am so sorry for your loss. Sorry for Caroline's loss. Sorry for my own loss. And mostly, sorry for Henry's loss."

A tear slid down Mrs. Crawford's cheek.

"I know she was everything to you, and memories of her are painful."

Mr. Crawford hadn't moved since Jason began speaking. Mrs. Crawford's shoulders heaved with silent sobs.

"I can't and won't pretend to imagine your

grief, and I apologize for causing you additional pain, but I know you love Henry, and if you want him to live to see his second birthday, we're going to need your help."

NINE

Jason didn't miss Caroline's sharp intake of breath. Mrs. Crawford choked on her sobs. Mr. Crawford leaned forward in his recliner. "Son, what on earth are you talking about?"

"I'm sorry to have to be so blunt, but in the past thirty-six hours, someone has tried to kill Caroline and Henry—"

"Kill?" Mrs. Crawford said with a gasp.

"Three times," Jason confirmed.

"Three?"

Might as well rip the Band-Aid off quick. "Yes. Three times. Caroline interrupted an intruder in her home on Thursday. He fired a weapon at them but then ran away. We hoped it was a random break-in." Not that he'd actually believed it to be random, even then. "But then we discovered that someone—probably the same someone—had tampered with the water heater. They were nearly overcome by carbon monoxide poisoning in the early hours of Friday morning. Then this morning, we discovered that someone had filled the seats in my Explorer—including Henry's car seat— with fire ants."

The fire ant attack bothered him. Getting past Caroline's alarm system and then sneaking the ants into Jason's car without leaving any trace behind proved that they were dealing with a pro. But why would a pro use such a random, ineffective means of attack? It didn't fit with the others.

"Mrs. Crawford." Caroline's soft voice broke, and she swallowed hard. "Stephanie was my best friend, and I would never want to say anything negative about her. I've tried to honor her request that we never search out Henry's birth father's family."

Mrs. Crawford's mouth flattened into a thin line. "I appreciate that, Caroline. I never want to know anything about that…that—"

"I don't, either, but we don't have a choice."

"Oh, yes, we do. I will not violate my daughter's last wishes. She must have had her reasons, and I don't need to know what they were to follow them."

Not good. "I'm sure she did," Jason said. "But it seems safe to assume her intention was to protect Henry. Unfortunately, in order to protect Henry, we now need to find out everything we can about the family. If Henry's being attacked because of his father, then we can't protect him without knowing why he's a target."

Mrs. Crawford shook her head back and forth. She sat straight and fixed a venomous glare, first in his direction, then Caroline's.

"No."

"Mrs. Crawf—"

"I said no." Mrs. Crawford stood. "I will not go against my daughter's wishes. I'm sorry someone has tried to harm you, and, of course, I don't want Henry hurt, but you can't even be sure this has anything to do with Henry's father."

She pointed at Caroline. "It's not like you've

never had issues at HPI. This could just as easily be the work of a disgruntled employee. I don't know why you're so determined to stick your noses where they don't belong, but you won't get any help from me."

Caroline's fingers flew to her throat. Her face was a mask of shock racing toward fury.

Mr. Crawford shifted in his seat. "Maybe we should talk about this another time," he said. His tone spoke of many years of peace-making experience.

"But—"

"That's probably best," Jason said, cutting Caroline off and earning himself a lethal look. He scooped Henry into his arms. "If you should think of anything that might help, you know how to reach us." He stretched his free hand to Caroline. She met his eyes, and he willed her to trust him. She pulled in a deep breath and took his hand, standing.

He tried to ignore the way her hand in his, combined with the weight of Henry on his other arm, satisfied some deep place he made a real effort to pretend didn't exist.

Once he had her moving toward the door, Caroline didn't waste time exiting the house. She stomped to the car but kept her thoughts to herself until Henry was strapped in and the doors closed on them.

Then she let them fly.

"What kind of woman would endanger her living, breathing grandson to try to protect the shreds of her very dead daughter's reputation?"

Jason turned the key in the ignition. As he backed out of the driveway, Mr. Crawford stepped onto the porch. It was hard to tell if he was angry or regretful.

Father, let it be regret.

Jason would give them a day. That was all he could afford. After that, he'd pay Mr. Crawford another visit. If they were going to get any information, it would come from him.

Caroline hadn't finished venting. "It's not like Steph's reputation wasn't in tatters already. She came home pregnant. Most people don't believe she was married. How can Mrs.

Crawford think digging into Henry's father's past will make people think anything worse?"

Jason let her stew for a few minutes. He hadn't forgotten how hot her temper burned, or how quickly the flame extinguished. At least that was how it used to be.

She stopped ranting but continued to glare out the passenger window. He could see the emotions playing across her features reflected in the glass. They'd almost reached his parents' driveway when she sighed.

"Stephanie's death devastated them," she said in a whisper. "For years, they thought they couldn't have children, and when she was born, she was the light in their world. They enjoy Henry, and I'm sure if she'd lived they would be the stereotypical doting grandparents, but…"

"But?"

"It's hard for them when he reminds them so much of her. Not in looks, really, but every now and then he does something and I see her. She's in his mannerisms more than his features. I think her parents pick up on it more than I do, and I think it causes them more pain than comfort. It happened with Steph, too, when she was still alive. Every now and then she'd look at Henry and she'd just look so sad. I knew she was thinking of her husband." She groaned. "I wonder how much Steph knew."

"Knew about what?"

"Henry's dad."

"I'm not following you."

"In the will. Her wishes were explicit. No contact was to be made with Henry's father's family. She never wanted him to know them, and she didn't want them to know him."

"Okay." Jason didn't want to point out that she'd told him all this already.

Caroline shifted in her seat, turning toward him. Her eyes no longer sparked with anger, but with excitement. "What if Stephanie knew Henry would be in danger from them? What if she suspected what would happen if his existence came to light?"

Jason parked the Explorer. She might be onto something. "But if Stephanie knew, why on earth wouldn't she have confided in you?

Why would she leave you without any way to know what's going on?"

"Maybe she planned to but didn't have a chance?"

Jason tried to remember everything he'd known about Stephanie. She'd been organized and thorough. "Or maybe she left you information and you haven't found it yet."

"What do you mean?"

"Did she leave you anything, Caroline? A note explaining things separate from the will?"

"Yes, but there's nothing—"

"Are you sure?"

Caroline narrowed her eyes at him. "You can read it if you like. Maybe you'll see something I missed."

"Where is it?"

"At my house."

He drummed his fingers on the steering wheel. "Was Stephanie living with her parents at the time of her death?"

"Oh, no. She had a cute little duplex."

"Where was it?"

"In town."

"So, when you got Henry, did the Crawfords give you his stuff from the duplex, or…"

Caroline fiddled with the bracelet on her arm. "I stayed there with him for a couple of days while we were figuring out what to do. It was all very confusing and upsetting, and we thought he'd feel better in a familiar environment. I had no idea she even had a will, much less that it was this complicated trust document. The attorney was nice, but all business. Kept going on about how Ms. Crawford had been quite clear about her wishes and he had drafted the documents in accordance with her requests."

Caroline mimicked a formal voice. "Ms. Crawford this and Ms. Crawford that. I still don't know how she was able to afford him. He's the definition of a high-priced attorney. Dad says he handles the trust and estate business of half the wealthy people in the county."

Jason fought the smile threatening to break across his face at the way Caroline said "the wealthy people in the county" without any indication that she was one of them.

Come to think of it, his birth father would fit that description, too. He might even use the same attorney. Jason's insides churned at the thought. His birth father had tried to call him off and on for the past several months. He'd ignored the calls, letting them go to voice mail, then deleting the messages unheard.

He rolled his head from one side to the other, fighting the way his neck tightened up at the thought of talking to the man who continued to cast a dark shadow on his life.

"Anyway," Caroline continued, "once we knew Henry was coming home to stay with me, we packed up his nursery and moved it to my house."

"Makes sense."

Caroline's eyes shimmered. "I hope he will always know how much she loved him. And how much I love him. I hope he grows up secure in that."

"He will," Jason said. "It's obvious to anyone how much you love him. You're a great mother, Caroline."

She gave him a sad smile. "Stephanie was much better. She had the most amazing scrapbooks for him. They're beautiful."

"Well, you can make him a scrapbook, can't you?"

"I can put pictures in an album. Stephanie was an artist. The pages are decorated with hand-drawn sketches, little notes to him, funny remarks about what he was doing..."

"I'd love to see them."

Caroline gave a harsh laugh. "Little chance of that. I doubt Mrs. Crawford will let you cross the threshold anytime soon."

"You don't have the albums?"

"No. Mrs. Crawford didn't want to part with any of Stephanie's stuff. Everything that wasn't baby related was boxed up and taken to the Crawfords. Steph's art studio is still set up in the basement with all her paintings and supplies, and I think they've turned it into a type of shrine to Stephanie. I think someday Henry might want it, especially her artwork, but I didn't want to upset Mrs. Crawford, and it's not like Henry wants any of it right now."

Jason grabbed her hand. "You mean you never went through Stephanie's stuff after she died?"

Caroline looked surprised. "Of course I did. I looked through her room and her desk. I needed insurance paperwork, birth certificates, etc. I took what I felt was applicable to Henry—"

"But you didn't search everything in her room, her studio?"

"Well, no. I—"

"The answers we need may be in her stuff. Stephanie might have left clues for you, or for Henry when he gets old enough to wonder about his father. Maybe there's a letter for Henry to read when he's older or a key to a safe-deposit box or, I don't know, something that will give us something to go on."

"You may be right, but we just ticked off the people who have possession of all of Stephanie's personal belongings. What are we going to do now?"

* * *

Caroline's mind wouldn't stop spinning.

"I should have searched through everything she owned," she said.

Jason stopped her. "Don't go there, Caroline. You had no reason to back then. Your focus was exactly where it needed to be—on Henry. I'm sure he spent quite a bit of time crying for his mommy."

He had. They'd cried together. Night after night. As she held his tiny body and wiped away his tears, she begged God to explain Himself. How could He have allowed this to happen? To her. To Henry. To Stephanie. What had any of them ever done to deserve to suffer this way?

She wasn't perfect. She'd messed up more times than she could count, but she was a good girl. She'd been in church her whole life. Accepted Christ as her Savior in elementary school. Never got in any trouble in high school. Dated a few morons, but she'd never really cared about them. None of them had ever been more than a distraction. An attempt to make Jason jealous.

Not that it had ever worked.

Even with Jason never seeing her as more than a buddy, she'd worked hard, gotten into Duke. Left for the university and thrown herself into college life.

She met Chad her sophomore year, and life had been perfect.

Until the day the police called. She'd identified his body. Even now, a decade later, her mind shied away from the image. His body mangled, thanks to a drunken driver.

At the funeral, the pastor said Chad's time on earth was ordained to be brief. Was that supposed to be comforting? Was that supposed to help her process how short his life was? Or how long her own stretched out in front of her without him?

She'd come home to grieve, and for a time she'd watched the days come and go without fully processing how they passed. She couldn't remember at what point they came to mean something again, but they did. Stephanie would stop by, make sure she was eating, force her to go to a movie with her or go shopping. Eventually, she started to look forward to the outings.

When she returned to school, she threw herself into her academics. If she was studying, she didn't have time to think about how the future she'd planned had ended before it had even begun.

After graduation, she began her work at Harrison Plastics International. She knew her father would have given her a job no matter what, but she wanted to earn the position. She wanted to make her dad proud. Her predecessor made no secret of the fact that he'd been waiting for her to graduate so she could take over and he could retire. He retired four months after she came on board.

And then things got really interesting. Life got busy and full. But she never really found the happy, fulfilled, loving future she'd always hoped and prayed for. God, it seemed, had other plans for her. She wished He'd let her in on them.

"Caroline?"

She looked at Jason's worried face.

"Are you okay?"

She wasn't, and she hadn't been for a long time. Not that she could tell Jason that. "I have to be," she said. "I'm all Henry has."

Jason squeezed her hand. "Caroline, you don't have to carry this alone."

"I carry everything alone," she said. "I know my family is here for me. I know they'll help me with anything, anytime. But I'm not wired to depend on others. I help everyone else. I don't know how to ask for help for myself."

"Then you need to learn," he said. His words weren't harsh. Each one was infused with compassion. "I'm still learning it myself, and I don't always get it right. If you don't feel like you can share with your family or your friends, you can always take it to God. He's always there. Always listening."

Caroline pulled her hand away. "I know that in my head. But my heart can't feel it. I believe He's Sovereign, but that means He knew this would happen, and He did nothing to stop it." She shrugged. "It's hard to trust someone who has let you down."

Pain shot across Jason's face.

She hadn't meant that as a slam against him, but it seemed that was how he'd taken it.

"Caroline, He hasn't let you down. *People* have let you down. You live in a fallen world where bad things happen. Friends die too young. Adults behave like children and children are forced to behave like adults." His eyes burned with regret. "I let you down. I left and I never tried to fix things between us. I thought it would be better that way, and then I felt guilty for handling it that way. I tried to talk to you that first Christmas—"

"And I told you I never wanted to speak to you again," Caroline said. "I was embarrassed. And I was hurt. I didn't mean it."

"I knew you didn't, but it was easier to take you at your word. Still, every time something big happened, I wanted to call. Send you an email. Something. But I didn't. I didn't call when Chad died. I didn't check on you after Blake's first wife went to jail. I didn't send a note when your dad had a stroke or when all that drama happened last year at the plant. I don't have an excuse. Neither do any of the other people who have failed you." He shifted his gaze, staring at nothing in particular. "People will fail you. He won't."

"You don't think God let you down when you were a kid and your—" She couldn't say it. She knew his birth father had a serious problem with alcohol, and when he was drunk, he was a mean drunk. What made it worse was that he was defensive about his drinking, refusing to admit he had a problem. That meant that no matter how out of control he got, he never let himself back down or apologize afterward for the cruel things he did while drinking. That led to a sort of stubborn combativeness that made everything worse.

Jason's mom had filed for divorce when Jason was one, but it had taken until he was three for it to be finalized. Even after she was able to get full custody, Jason's birth father would argued with Jason's mom over everything from where Jason went to elementary school to what brand tennis shoes he wore. And he'd humiliated Jason more than once as he yelled at the coaches and players while Jason played ball. He claimed he was acting out of love and concern, but it seemed more like spite and wounded ego. He'd been a constant trial during Jason's childhood.

"I think my father was an idiot," Jason said. "I still do. And I'm still working through how I'm supposed to deal with him as an adult." He glanced at his phone. He'd ignored five calls from his birth father in the past three days. "But I don't blame God for any of that. My father made bad choices, and I had to live with them. But my mom found the strength to get out. Then she found the courage to risk loving again, and I got the dad I'd always dreamed of. And of course, that's when I met you. They got married and we moved here the summer before I started kindergarten. I remember you and your mom brought brownies and that was the start of our families' friendship. So, it wasn't all bad."

Caroline appreciated his attempt to put a

positive spin on things, but his dad's health crisis loomed in her mind.

"I know you're thinking about Dad," he said.

Scary how good he was at reading her mind. "Your dad, your career, your future—nothing's exactly turning out the way you wanted." How could he not be angry, or at least frustrated with God?

He smiled. "Yeah. It stinks. All of it. This isn't what I'd planned. Not even close. But I have peace that God is working, even in the mess, the pain, the loss. I don't understand what He's up to, but I am confident He is up to something."

He spoke with such sincerity. Such maturity.

When had Jason Drake grown up?

TEN

Jason couldn't figure out the look Caroline was giving him? Admiration? Annoyance? Both?

Regardless, he needed to change the subject. He knew from experience that trying to push someone into giving up their frustration with the Almighty didn't work.

He'd have to trust that the Almighty could take care of that for Himself.

"I have an idea," he said.

"What?" Skepticism laced her voice.

"Let's go back to your house and look through everything you have from Stephanie—everything the Crawfords didn't claim."

"I don't think there's anything there."

"There may not be, but we have to look. Sometimes things that appear innocuous take on a whole new meaning when you view them through a different lens."

She smirked. "What comes after that?"

"I'll have to talk to my boss. It might be possible for us to get a warrant to search through Stephanie's things."

"Are you crazy? Like the Crawfords don't hate us enough as it is?"

He shoved away the reaction his stomach had every time she referred to them as "we" and "us."

"I don't think it will come to that," he said. "Mr. Crawford looked like there were things he would have said if Mrs. Crawford hadn't been in such a state."

Caroline narrowed her eyes at him. "Really?"

"Don't be so pessimistic," he said. "I think there's a good chance he'll offer to help us as long as we catch him at the right moment."

"And by right moment, you mean when Mrs. Crawford isn't home?"

He laughed. "Something like that."

"That might be tough. They don't have an active social calendar."

"No, but Mrs. Crawford is planning to go to lunch with a friend tomorrow."

"How on earth do you know that?"

"They have a calendar on their fridge."

"Were you snooping in their house?"

"I wouldn't call it snooping."

"What would you call it?"

"Investigating."

Caroline laughed.

"I was hoping there might be a photo of Stephanie with a guy or in a unique location. Something that would give us a clue. I think there's a good chance I could go back tomorrow and talk to Mr. Crawford without Mrs. Crawford being around."

"Did you see anything else useful?" She sounded impressed.

"No." Not one single thing.

"Do you think we can safely reenter my house?"

"As soon as your sister-in-law's guy gives us the all clear, we'll head over there. I'm sure you'd like to sleep in your own bed tonight." Caroline didn't reply immediately. "Am I wrong?"

"No," she rushed to say. "I desperately want to be home, but I…I want to be home the way I was three days ago. I want to feel safe. It's always been my sanctuary. The place where everything is okay. Now it feels like my refuge has turned on me." She laughed at herself. "I know that sounds stupid."

"No, it doesn't," he said. "It's a normal reaction. Maybe even a mild form of post-traumatic stress syndrome."

She groaned.

"What?"

"I just realized what this means," she said.

He had no idea where she was going with this. "What does it mean?"

"Heidi's best friend, Sara, is a clinical psychologist who specializes in PTSD. Heidi experienced a lot of trauma as a kid, and Sara's helped her with that. Then last year, when Maggie was kidnapped by that lunatic at the plant, Sara came immediately. She's been unofficially seeing Maggie at least once a month ever since. I don't think Maggie even realizes she's in therapy. But Sara's done wonders for her." She blew out a long breath. "I've always suspected that Sara would love to get me on her couch. I guess she's about to get her chance."

"There's no shame in getting therapy," he said as he parked in front of his parents' house.

She studied him long enough to make him uncomfortable. He didn't see anger or frustration in her expression. He saw concern. Maybe understanding?

She started to speak a few times but stopped herself.

"Spit it out," he said.

"No," she said. "No, not now. Later."

"What's wrong with now?"

Her eyes flashed a warning a millisecond before his mother's voice stretched across the yard. "Jason Drake!"

He opened the door. "Yes, ma'am?"

"Are you two going to stay out there all afternoon? Bring that child in here!" As she stepped off the porch, he heard her mutter, "If someone's trying to kill you, seems like it would be safer to be in the house rather than sitting out in the open. But what do I know? I wasn't a sniper. I wasn't a marine. Nope. Not me. Just a housewife who watches too many cop shows, I guess."

Caroline laughed under her breath. "Your mom is a trip."

"Yeah," he said. "She has a PhD in sarcasm."

"She's worried, that's all."

That wasn't all. She *was* worried, but she was also hoping for something that couldn't happen. He walked behind Caroline, Henry held secure in her arms, probably looking to an outside observer like every inch the family his mother hoped they'd become.

No. It couldn't happen. No matter how much his mother wanted it.

Caroline watched Jason for the next couple of hours. He played with Henry, teased his mom and had a few conversations with his dad that didn't appear, on the surface, to have anything to do with her, but she suspected there was a subtext she wasn't quite following.

Regardless, when Jason's phone buzzed, her stomach did a flip, and she forced herself to breathe. He looked at his phone, then at her.

"Heidi says she has an agent at your house and he's given it the all clear. Unofficially, of course. She says you know the agent and that we should head over there to talk to him."

She took another breath. She should be relieved. She *was* relieved. Wasn't she?

"Did she say who it was?" This not-having-a-phone thing was getting really old, really fast.

"No. How many FBI agents do you know?"

"A few."

"Let's go see what the FBI unofficially has to say."

It took longer to get Henry buckled into his car seat than it did to reach her driveway. Jason punched in the security code, and as the gate slid open, her stomach clenched. If she lived through this mess, would she ever be able to approach her own home without fear? Would it ever feel safe?

Jason bumped her elbow. "Earth to Caroline. You okay?"

She hoped her smile was convincing. "Of course."

Jason sighed. So maybe her smile hadn't been as convincing as she'd hoped. They wound up the drive, past Blake and Heidi's, past her parents' home and on to the top of the mountain.

The red Camaro in her driveway eased her tension. She didn't realize she'd leaned forward in the seat until Jason said, "I guess you know this agent."

"Yes."

Kyle Richards stepped off the porch, hands on his waist. "Took you long enough," he said as he opened her door. He pulled her into a hug and squeezed her tight. "You okay?" he said into her hair.

She stepped out of his arms. "I'm good."

His mouth flattened into a tight line. "Not good enough," he said with a shake of his head. "This should never have happened. I am so sorry."

"None of this is your fault, Kyle."

"That's debatable." He looked like he wanted to say more, but his eyes flickered to Jason, now standing a mere two feet away.

She hesitated. Jason already knew Kyle was an agent. But how much could she say? She decided to stick with names and let Kyle take the lead. "Jason, I'd like you to meet Kyle Richards."

Kyle extended his hand and Jason shook it. "Jason Drake."

They nodded at each other. Sizing each other up, no doubt.

Caroline bumped Kyle's arm. "What are you doing here?"

"What do you think I'm doing here? I'm figuring out how that jerk got in your house."

"No, I mean I thought you were working. How did you get loose?"

"Heidi called."

Caroline blew out an exasperated breath.

"So I gathered, but there isn't supposed to be anything official about any—"

He lifted a hand, and she stopped talking. Had she spoken out of turn? She didn't want to ask Jason to leave, but it would be so much easier to talk to Kyle if she didn't have to worry about blowing his cover or whatever he called it.

Her family had been drawn into the shadowy world of covert operations a year and a half ago when the FBI sent her now sister-in-law, Heidi Zimmerman, to find out why the son of an organized crime family had landed a job at Harrison Plastics International. Heidi had ended up uncovering an elaborate crime ring with a deeply sinister plot. Heidi had done a brilliant job—but she hadn't done it alone. She'd had a whole team working with her.

That experience had left Caroline with the utmost respect for the dangers the FBI agents faced, and she took protecting their identities seriously. Not that Jason would ever pose a danger to Kyle, but it wasn't her place to reveal more than Kyle wanted.

"I'm just doing a friend a favor," he said and winked at her.

Jason pulled in a slow breath. "Look, man, in case you haven't been brought up to speed, someone broke in here, bypassed a security system put in by the FBI and then nearly killed Caroline and Henry. We don't have time for games."

Caroline couldn't believe he'd said that. "Jason!"

"What? You two obviously know each other well, but I don't know this guy and I don't care if he's here officially or not. What I want to know is how well he knows this system and what makes him think that it's secure now when it wasn't a few days ago."

The hostility in his words rocked Caroline.

"Kyle's the one who installed this system, and if you'd give him a chance, I'm sure he could answer your questions without all the drama."

"Forgive me, but if he's the one who installed it, then that makes him a prime suspect in my book."

"Jason."

Jason shook his head. "You've been telling me how awesome this system is. How no one can hack into it. Then the guy who installed it shows up and tells you it's safe now? Sorry. I'm not buying it. He could be the very one who created the back door your attacker used to get in."

What was his problem?

Kyle had yet to respond to Jason's accusations, and she turned her attention to him, worried that she'd find him upset and offended. Instead, a smile flickered across his face.

He straightened to his full six feet four inches and winked at Caroline before focusing on Jason. "It's okay, Caroline. He's worried. My guess is you told him you don't have a boyfriend. He believed you. Now he's not so sure."

She looked between the two of them. "What does that have to do with anything?"

Jason's skin had flushed at Kyle's taunt. Wait. Was Jason…jealous? Of Kyle?

Kyle shrugged. "I'm not so sure it's a good idea for the lead investigator on the case to be smitten with the victim, but I guess that's how things roll in small-town America."

"Are you questioning my professionalism?" Jason didn't yell, but the strain in his voice frightened her more than if he'd been screaming.

"You just accused me of being behind the attacks on Caroline. Are you saying that was a professional accusation?"

Caroline stepped between the two men.

"Would you listen to yourselves? This is ridiculous." She turned to Jason. "Kyle is now a part of our extended family." She turned to Kyle. "Jason has been my best friend since kindergarten."

Her words seemed to surprise both men, and some of the tension eased. Slightly.

"Let's start over," she said.

They eyed each other.

"Now."

After what felt like an hour, Jason stretched out his hand. "Jason Drake." Kyle shook his hand. It looked like they might have been squeezing a little harder than necessary, but at least they weren't fighting.

"If it keeps Caroline safe, I'll take any help I can get." Jason cut his eyes at Caroline, and she saw a trace of humor in them. "Even if it means dealing with the unofficial FBI."

Kyle nodded. "Well, if I'm going to be fair," he admitted, "your accusations aren't entirely unfounded. You're asking good questions. They're ridiculous, of course, but they are fair."

Boys. Men. Idiots.

Still, she trusted both of them to keep her safe. Or try to, anyway.

"Kyle, I know you didn't have anything to do with this," she said.

He laughed. "I appreciate that, but if the roles were reversed, I'd be asking the same questions. This system…" His voice trailed off, his frustration evident.

Henry let out a little cry, his own frustration at being left in his car seat bubbling to the surface. Poor baby. All he'd done for the past two days was get in and out of stupid car seats. When this was over, she was going to stay home for a week. A month.

Before she could get to Henry, Jason pulled the door open and had him unfastened faster than she'd expected. "Sorry, buddy. Let's get you inside. I bet you're ready to be home, aren't you, little man?"

Henry was laughing as Jason settled him in his arms. "Do you want the diaper bag?"

"Nah. It can stay in the car."

He carried Henry to the house, and her breathing hitched as she watched them. Henry needed a daddy.

Where had that come from? This paternal side of Jason was messing with her. Henry did need a daddy, but Jason Drake certainly wouldn't be signing up for the job. He'd made his feelings about having children, living in North Carolina and having a relationship with her clear a long time ago.

Well, it *had* been clear.

Now?

Now she had no idea what was going on.

ELEVEN

Three hours later, as Caroline settled Henry into his bed for the night, Jason excused himself from the living room. He didn't know how much more he could take of Kyle.

Caroline might not realize it, but that guy was in love with her.

He let himself onto the porch, stepped to the rail and pulled in a slow breath through his nose, then blew it out through his mouth.

Be fair, Drake. Caroline's a great girl. Gorgeous. Sweet. Wealthy. The guy would have to be dead not to be interested in her.

Besides, why did he care? What had changed in the past decade?

Not her. Well, not in any negative way. She was a little quieter than he remembered.

Not quite so fiery, although the temper was still there.

Her hair was longer, and her body a little curvier than it had been at eighteen, but the years had been good to her. The only thing about her that had truly aged was her eyes.

When he looked into her eyes, he didn't see the carefree girl of his childhood.

He saw a woman who'd borne her share of grief. A woman who'd survived tragedy and trauma and come out on the other side of them stronger. He saw a woman who knew who she was and what she wanted, and he had no doubt that her roles as business leader and mother would trump any other role she might consider.

Like wife.

He shook his head. Time to get off this merry-go-round. He'd let it drive him crazy in high school. The wondering. The maybe. The what if she cared? The bottom line hadn't changed. Her world was here.

But as long as his birth father was here, he couldn't be.

He couldn't imagine a life where that man constantly picked apart his every decision. He couldn't imagine subjecting a woman he loved to that man's derision and interference. And what if they did have children? How could he put any child through what he'd gone through?

The image of his birth father showing up to a Little League game or a piano recital drunk, loud and refusing to leave quietly burned in his brain.

No. He'd get her through this, get his mom and dad through the next few years, and then he'd be gone.

Again.

Her life was here, and she deserved so much more than he would ever be able to give. He knew he was right about this, so why couldn't he stop wondering about what it would be like to be proved wrong?

The door opened behind him. Kyle. Great. Just who he wanted to see.

"I need you inside." Kyle glared into the darkness before locking the door behind Jason.

"What's wrong?"

"I don't know. I set up the system to alert me to any movement on the property."

Jason pulled his gun out. Caroline's eyes were hooded.

"You did that in one day?" Jason asked. He didn't want to be impressed, but one day?

Kyle's fingers flew over the keyboard of his laptop. He grunted. "My team did it in one dark, rainy, cold night." He winked at Caroline. Jason ignored the temptation to tackle him to the ground.

"The capability has been here since last year, but we haven't been monitoring it for months. I reestablished all the connections this afternoon. I've got cameras running, and some of them even have microphones."

"So what are we dealing with?"

"I'm not sure yet. Got a hit from the motion sensors on the edge of the property near the plant. That's the easiest place for someone to access this mountain without having to hike through thick forest half the day."

Kyle continued to scan a variety of windows on his laptop screen.

Caroline paced the floor.

Jason prayed. *Father, whatever's coming our way, give us wisdom, protect us, especially Caroline.*

He had to hand it to Kyle, not that he wanted to, but the guy's expression was glacial. No hesitation. No doubt. No indication of fear. Nothing but cold determination that whoever had dared set foot on this property wouldn't be stepping off it until they knew why he'd come.

Kyle's eyes narrowed, and he leaned toward the screen. "I've got you now, you..." His voice trailed off. "There." He pointed at the screen. "Do you see it?"

Jason looked at the small window. He saw nothing but darkness. But then the darkness fluttered. "Was that—"

"Yep."

"Was that what?" Caroline's words were thick with tension.

He tried to explain. "I can't make out exactly what I'm seeing, but something in the darkness moved. And I think—" he squinted his eyes at the screen "—I think the motion is coming from above the ground. Maybe someone's in a tree?"

Kyle nodded. "I think so, too."

Not a sniper. Please, not a sniper.

Kyle turned in his chair and looked at him. "What do you think?"

Jason swallowed hard. "I think I'd better go check it out."

"Not alone!" Caroline's face had paled.

He appreciated the concern, but what choice did they have?

"Caroline, we can't leave you and Henry alone."

"I can protect myself," she said.

Kyle snorted.

"I don't appreciate that attitude, Kyle Richards. I am a grown woman and I know how to use a gun."

Kyle held up his hands in surrender. "I'm not saying you aren't or you don't. But if you think either one of us would be willing to leave you in here by yourself, you're crazier than I thought you were. You can get mad if you want, but there's no way we're both going."

He looked at Jason. "I don't see any way to get backup in here without spooking him. But I think we should have them on standby."

Jason nodded. "I'll make the call."

Jason pulled his phone from his pocket. Probably calling Mike, Caroline thought. Maybe Mike would talk some sense into him.

He could not go after this guy alone. Could. Not. No way he was going out there by himself. She wouldn't allow it.

They could wait for backup.

Then the backup could go after this intruder. While Jason stayed right here where she could see him.

What did it say about her that she would risk others' lives but not his? No. She wouldn't go there. Not now. She couldn't.

But if he stepped outside…

"Wait!" The idea wasn't fully formed, but it was an idea. A little bit of one, anyway.

Kyle shook his head at the screen but didn't

look away from it. Jason quirked one eyebrow, but she could tell he was humoring her. He was ready to go out there. She'd better talk fast.

"We haven't had supper."

She saw incredulity cross both men's faces. "Hear me out!"

Jason dropped the mask of determination he'd been wearing. "What are you thinking?"

"Have the backup come in as pizza delivery. Surely Mike can get the guys at the Pizza Shack to let him borrow one of their cars. He could pull up, take the curves super slow, let a few guys out on the driveway near Mom and Dad's, then come here with a pizza box."

She watched them process the information. Kyle blinked at the screen several times before saying, "Might work."

Jason's face was easier to read. Was that because he wasn't as trained as Kyle was at keeping up the mask, or was it because he was Jason and she'd always known what he was thinking? Well, usually.

Regardless, she could tell he was giving her

idea some serious thought. She knew the moment he decided. He put the phone back to his ear. "Michael," he said, then laughed. "Oh, you heard her idea, huh?" A few moments of silence while Jason nodded and paced the room. Would it kill him to put the phone on speaker? Finally, he winked at her. "See you in twenty. Be careful."

He slid the phone in his pocket. "Michael's on it. A couple of guys on patrol are already headed this way. They won't pull into the driveway, but they'll be close enough to come in with sirens blaring if we need them. We have a guy who we've sent undercover a couple of times on alcohol sales stings. He looks sixteen. He'll come in with the pizza. I'll change into his clothes and go back out."

"Why do you have to go?" Caroline tried to keep the panic out of her voice. "Let one of the other guys do the search."

Jason was shaking his head in disagreement. "I know this mountain better than the others do. I can't ask them to take a risk in an unfamiliar environment when I can help them."

Caroline wanted to argue, but she couldn't.

Jason glanced in Kyle's direction. Kyle nodded. "I like the plan. When they head this way, tell them to be sure to stop at the gate and request us to open it. If they just drive in, it might clue the guy that something's up." His lips twitched, and he flicked a quick look in her direction. "Unless the Pizza Shack guys know the code."

"They most certainly do not," she said. They used to, before Heidi entered their lives. Not anymore.

Jason excused himself with a "Be right back." She watched him until he stepped into the hall bathroom.

When she looked back toward Kyle, he was watching her. His smile was soft, almost tender. And somehow…resigned? "So, that's Jason, huh?" His voice was so low she knew Jason couldn't hear them.

"What's that supposed to mean?" She'd never spoken of Jason to Kyle. She rarely spoke of Jason to anyone. Blake got all sullen whenever she mentioned him. No one could hold a grudge like a big brother.

She'd told Heidi about him once. Heidi had been sympathetic toward both of them. Had even said that expecting an eighteen-year-old boy to behave rationally was like expecting a Brit to skip afternoon tea. It might happen occasionally, but it certainly couldn't be counted on.

When they found out he'd moved back to town, Heidi hadn't said a word to Caroline. Just gave her a long look. She'd been expecting her sister-in-law to bring him up, but she hadn't yet.

But she knew with certainty that she'd never mentioned Jason to Kyle, and she didn't believe Heidi would have.

Kyle didn't answer her question. "Kyle?"

He shook his head. "It means I've always known there was someone. Just didn't know who he was. Now that I do, I can see how futile it is to try to convince you to think of anyone else."

What was he saying? He wasn't…was he?

He turned back to the screen. "You're in love with him. I don't know what the history is, but you might consider giving the guy a fighting chance. You'll always be happier with the one you were made for than trying to make someone who was never intended for you work."

Was he talking to her, or himself?

"Of course, if he turns out to be an idiot, call me. I'll be happy to try to make you forget him."

Heat flooded every square inch of her skin at his implication. Heidi had said Kyle had a crush on her, but she hadn't believed it. Why would he choose to confess it now? And what was he picking up on in her actions that would make him believe she was in love with Jason?

The bathroom door opened, and Jason looked from her face to the back of Kyle's head. "Did I miss something?"

Caroline said, "No."

Kyle said, "We'll see."

Jason looked between the two of them. She shook her head, silently imploring him to drop it. If the circumstances had been different, he probably wouldn't have.

But with a stranger sitting in a tree a few hundred yards from the house and a bunch of cops headed their way in a pizza delivery car, maybe he decided this wasn't the best time to hash things out.

When she looked up, Jason was much closer than she'd expected. He leaned in, his hand on her elbow. "Things may get a little dicey. Why don't you check on Henry?"

Henry slept in peace. How she envied him. She left his room and crept to her bathroom, not turning on the lights as she went. She was sure her rapid pulse was due to the danger they were in. Nothing more. The tingles that spread through her arms as Jason touched her were due to her nerves. Not because his hand lingered on her arm a few seconds longer than necessary.

She wouldn't let Kyle's intimations worm their way into her mind.

She'd gotten over Jason a long time ago. She'd had to. She wasn't a moonstruck teenager. Her emotions wouldn't get away from her again.

When she returned to the living room, Jason and Kyle hovered over the laptop. "Here they come." Kyle pointed to a small box on the far right of his screen. "Want me to open the gate from here?"

"Sure."

Jason looked like a kid getting ready to go to an amusement park. Not like a grown man heading into an unknown and potentially deadly situation.

How could he be looking forward to this?

When the doorbell rang, she forced her feet to stay still. Jason was right. The officer who stepped through her door could easily pass for a teenager. He didn't mess around. He placed the pizza box on the table and slid out of the jacket and hat he was wearing. When he started unbuttoning his shirt, Caroline looked away.

What was he doing?

The sound of Velcro straps being pulled apart drew her attention back.

A bulletproof vest.

Panic enveloped her. *Oh, God, please don't let anything happen to Jason.*

Where had that come from? Did she really think He'd let her keep anything she loved?

She watched in mute fascination as Jason secured the vest over his shirt, then pulled the jacket and hat on. Up close, the disguise was thin, but in the dark, from a distance, it might work.

Might.

What had she done?

He could be shot the second he stepped through the door.

The young officer walked over to where Kyle sat, both of them now engrossed in the images on the screen.

Kyle looked at Jason. "Be careful out there, Drake." He patted the arsenal of weapons that now surrounded him. "We'll keep them safe."

"Thanks, man."

He moved toward the front door.

She lost her battle with her feet. "Jason."

She fought to keep her voice steady. "Please be careful."

She expected him to wink at her. Throw a quick grin her way and skip out the door.

Instead, he turned, his eyes boring into hers. He closed the distance between them in half a breath, and before her mind caught up with what was happening, his lips crashed into hers.

Their meeting was brief but fierce.

She didn't even consider pushing him away. He released her far too soon and pressed his forehead to hers, his chest heaving. "Just in case," he whispered. Then he was gone.

TWELVE

The cool of the evening air smacked Jason's overheated skin.

What had he just done?

That… That…

That was awesome.

He'd deal with the repercussions later.

Head in the game, Drake.

He got into the car, slid behind the driver's seat and eased his way down the driveway. "You okay?" he asked the young officer folded up like origami in the passenger seat.

"Yeah." The guy laughed. "The others are waiting for you past the turnoff to the senior Harrisons' house. Stop there."

"Thanks, man."

When they reached the designated spot, Jason threw the car into Park and darted from the car. The officer had it back in gear and rolling down the driveway in seconds. Hopefully no one noticed the brief delay.

How he wished there'd been a way to get wired into Richards up at the house. They were flying mostly blind. Richards had his cell number, but he would use it only in an emergency. Couldn't risk giving away his position.

He glanced around as he joined Michael and the other officers. Tomorrow, Richards was going to point out every camera on the property. For now, he had to hope Richards could see them.

He stripped out of the brightly colored pizza delivery guy costume and pulled on the tactical jacket Michael handed him.

They conferred in whispers for a few moments before heading out. The plan was to come at the guy from behind. If he ran, they would have a few officers forming a perimeter.

They didn't have enough people to prevent him from making an escape if he knew the property well, but it was the best they could do on such short notice.

The officers followed him. He wasn't the most senior officer at the scene, but he could only assume Michael had told them that he'd practically grown up on this mountain. He and Caroline had roamed every inch of this place as kids.

He tried to go on instinct. To let the muscle memory take over and lead him on the easiest path to their destination.

It worked…for the most part. He'd forgotten about that random bamboo stand until they were on top of it and had to go around it. But at least he'd known which direction to go to bypass it.

He lifted a closed fist, and everyone stopped moving. If their target hadn't moved, he should be a few hundred yards ahead, up in a pine. Hopefully facing the house and not expecting anyone to be coming from behind in the dark woods.

A crashing branch split the night air. It came from the opposite direction from where they'd paused. Was it one of the other officers? Was it their bad guy?

Or was it nothing more than a tree branch that fell to the forest floor by itself?

There was no way to know at the moment.

He pulled out his night vision binoculars and scanned the trees.

Yes. There.

He removed the binoculars and shielded his phone under his jacket to check the screen. Richards had texted him. No changes. No motion that was unaccounted for.

This guy seemed to be alone.

Not that being alone was the same as being harmless. He was probably the one who had broken into Caroline's home, tampered with her water heater, taken a shot at her and Henry, and maybe even the one who put the fire ants in Jason's car.

On his signal, one officer moved to his left. Michael was on his right, and another officer took a position fifty feet to Michael's right.

They closed in on the trespasser. With the

night vision goggles, he could see they all had their weapons trained on the intruder.

He and Michael continued to approach. They were within twenty feet when the guy jerked to a standing position and turned in their direction. He and Michael had both settled in behind large pines. In the darkness, it would be hard to make out their positions if you didn't know where to look.

Time for action. *Father, protect us.*

"You're surrounded." He didn't yell. The guy could hear him easily in the stillness of the night, and he wanted this to go smoothly. "Keep your hands where we can see them and climb down from the tree."

His pulse pounded in his ears while he waited. "Come on, man," he said. "This can end right now. No one needs to get hurt tonight."

Was his hand—

"Gun!" The cry came from both sides. Before he could react, an arm shot out.

"Grenade!"

There wasn't time to question whether it

was a genuine grenade or a flash bang. Jason ripped the night vision goggles off and caught a blur of motion as their target threw himself to the ground. The guy was making a run for it!

An explosion rocked the mountainside. Quickly followed by another. Jason's ears rang, but he was otherwise unharmed. He rose, crouching behind a tree.

Had the intruder had time to flee? Had he gotten through their pitiful defense in the confusion?

A yell. A shot!

He ran in the direction of the sound. The most important thing now was to be sure no one on his team accidentally hurt anyone through friendly fire. Running around in the dark with loaded weapons was a dangerous way to spend the evening.

He paused behind a tree. The intruder must have night vision goggles. He could be anywhere. Where would he have gone? *Think, Drake. Think.*

He pulled in a few steadying breaths.

Ah. Yes.

He darted from tree to tree, not in a straight line, but zigzagging his way in the direction of the bamboo. If their target was there, he'd need to sneak up on him. The last thing he wanted was for the guy to start lobbing grenades at them again.

Who did that? Grenades?

He waited. Seconds felt like hours as he scanned the edge of the bamboo. All he could do was hope Richards could see him and would communicate with his men.

Why hadn't they figured out a better plan for what to do if the whole thing blew up in their faces?

He knew why. Limited resources. Even more limited time.

Still, there was nothing quite like planning an operation that turns into a complete bust, all while you've got an FBI agent watching your every move.

He hated looking like an idiot.

Hated looking like an idiot in front of the

FBI even more. Especially that particular FBI agent.

He didn't even want to think about what Kyle would be saying to Caroline right now. Probably giving her a breakdown of every way Jason had mangled this evening's adventure and how he would have done it differently, better.

Head in the game, Drake. Focus.

Five minutes later, he saw it. Years ago, there'd been a narrow path in the bamboo. Jason hadn't bothered looking for it on their way in. It wouldn't have been wide enough for the group of them to move through silently. But one man could do it. Especially if he knew it was there.

If this guy knew the path, he'd been spending a lot of time on this mountain.

It was time for him to tell them why.

Jason made his way around the perimeter of the bamboo. There it was. The opening. If their perp was in that bamboo, he'd have to come out from there.

He didn't have to wait long. In the darkness,

the intruder darted from the bamboo, straight to a tree. He crouched behind it.

Jason didn't have time to plan his next move. He stepped to the other side of the tree and aimed his weapon. "You move your arms anywhere but straight up, and I'll drop you."

Slowly, both arms stretched into the night sky.

Jason held his position.

"Michael?"

"Right behind you."

Michael's voice came from behind him and to the left.

"We're here, too," said another voice. Jason would have to find out what their names were as soon as this was over.

He approached the intruder. Michael stepped close to cover him as he returned his gun to his holster. "You are under arrest for trespassing and for assaulting an officer."

"I didn't know you were cops."

Jason grabbed the guy's arms and handcuffed him faster than he'd ever handcuffed anyone before. As soon as he was done, Michael frisked the guy.

"What do you mean you didn't know we were cops? Who were you expecting?"

The guy shook his head. "Nope. Not talking. I know my rights. I want a lawyer."

"You out here alone?"

The guy looked at the officers surrounding him. "Obviously not."

A smart aleck. Awesome.

Michael took one arm while Jason took the other. The flashing lights of the cars pierced through the trees as they made their way back to the driveway and the waiting backup.

They secured him in the back of the car and patted the hood. "That was ridiculous," Michael said. "How'd you know he'd be in there?"

"Had a hunch," he said.

"It was a good one. When everyone scattered, we pulled back to the house. Richards could see where you were and Caroline told us about the path in the bamboo. So we came back out after you."

"I'm glad you did, man." He patted Michael on the back. "Let's go find out who this guy is."

Michael nodded. "I'll ride back to the station with Jarod."

Jarod. One name down, one to go.

Michael nodded toward the house. "You may be a few minutes. I'll start getting him processed."

Yeah. He'd acted recklessly. More than once tonight. Time to pay the piper. "Right. I'll go get my car."

Caroline couldn't stop herself from pacing as she waited for Jason to come back to the house. Her emotions were all over the place.

He had some nerve. Daring to kiss her.

And that was no friendly peck. He'd kissed her until she could barely remember where she was, then he walked into the darkness and almost got blown up by a grenade—two of them. Then, when he was supposed to pull back to the house, he had to go all superhero and track the guy into a stand of bamboo.

She was going to kill him.

Or kiss him.

It could go either way, and that was a big problem. There could be no more kissing. None. She stomped down the driveway. If he'd left without speaking to her—

He rounded the curve at a light jog, and she skidded to a stop.

Now what?

Her legs tried to bolt toward him. Her arms seemed to think wrapping themselves around him would be a good idea right about now. Holding on and never letting—

No.

Her mind regained control. She crossed her arms. There would be no more shenanigans. If he thought he could waltz back into her life like this and play games with her heart, he was mistaken.

"What's wrong?"

He had *not* just asked her that. "What's wrong? Are you kidding me?"

He stepped closer. "Are you okay? Is Henry—"

The obvious concern, both for her and her

son, stopped her in her tracks. And chipped away at her anger. "We're fine. Henry slept through the whole thing."

Relief washed over his features, then confusion. "Did you need something?"

"Did I what?"

"You chased me down the driveway, Caroline. Did you need something?"

Oops. "I wanted to make sure you were okay. You disappeared from the camera view for a while."

Wow. That was pitiful. But she couldn't very well tell him the truth. That her need to see him alive and whole, for herself and not through an infrared camera lens, made no rational sense.

She didn't have the time or energy to process everything that had happened tonight.

"Oh." Was he disappointed in her answer?

Why did that make her heart flip?

"I need to get my car," he said, continuing his climb up her driveway. He seemed determined to pretend that the kiss hadn't happened. Fine. She could do that, too. She fell into step beside him.

"What happens next?" There. That was a perfectly rational question.

"We interview him. Tonight. As soon as they get him processed."

"How long will it take to process him?"

"A couple of hours. We have to have him checked out by a nurse. Offer him food, water, a lawyer."

"Can you talk to him without the lawyer?"

"We can talk. He may not answer. The main thing will be to see what we can learn about him from his prints. A guy like this is bound to have a record somewhere. But it's not like it is on TV. We don't have a hacker who can get us into supersecret FBI files." He bumped her elbow with his. "Although I'm hoping Kyle might be able to help us with that. Unofficially, of course."

"Of course," she said. They both laughed, and the tension lessened.

This was how it was supposed to be between them. Easy. Conversational. A little sarcasm thrown in for good measure.

"Kyle probably knows a thing or two about hacking," she said. "Unofficially."

"Of course." He laughed. "I'm sure Kyle will do anything he can to help you." She didn't miss the implication in his tone. Was Kyle right about him? About them?

She pulled in a deep breath. She couldn't think about it anymore. Nothing was making sense.

"You need to sleep," he said.

"So do you."

"I'll sleep when it's over."

"If you don't get some sleep, it may be over for you before you want it to be."

He snorted. "I'll get some sleep soon, but you need to get some now. Kyle's on alert. This mountain is crawling with cops. Whatever this guy was up to, he's done for the night. Might as well rest up now."

She wanted to argue, but her eyelids begged her to listen.

They reached his car. His hand closed over hers in the darkness. He cleared his throat.

If he tried to kiss her again—

"I'll call you as soon as I know something. Until then, stay close to Kyle. Don't leave the house or go wandering around in the woods. I'll be back soon." He squeezed her hand and slid behind the wheel. The window inched down. "I'm not leaving until you go inside, Caroline."

His voice held so much tenderness. Why was he being so protective? So nice? She wanted to despise him, but he was making it difficult.

"Right," she said with what she hoped sounded like a carefree laugh. No way could he know what he was doing to her.

She jogged to the house. The door opened as she approached. That was when she remembered what she was sure Jason had not forgotten.

The cameras.

Kyle.

Watching.

Even as a teenager, Jason had been the perfect gentleman. Opening doors. Standing when a lady was present. Holding chairs and sweaters and umbrellas. That hadn't changed.

And a gentleman wouldn't kiss a lady—especially when he wasn't sure if she wanted to be kissed—with an audience.

She lay down on the trundle bed in Henry's room. If the cameras hadn't been there, would he have kissed her again?

If he had tried, would she have let him?

Her mind didn't like the answer her heart supplied.

THIRTEEN

Jason entered the detention center and nodded at the deputy behind the desk.

"Your boy is a real charmer," the officer said.

"Giving you a hard time?" Jason didn't break his stride. This guy complained about everyone who walked in the door. He'd thought of him as "Negative Ned" so much, he had a hard time remembering his real name.

"Scared out of his mind is more like it. Keeps saying we've sentenced him to death. That they'll kill him."

Jason backtracked. He leaned across the desk. Talbert. That was it. Joe Talbert. "What exactly did he say?"

Talbert shrugged. "I didn't write it down, man. I don't have time for that mess. Guy gets caught peeping into Caroline Harrison's window? He probably figures that brother of hers will kill him. Might be right about that. I hear Blake Harrison can handle himself."

Blake was more than capable of handling himself, but Jason didn't believe for a second that their perp was worried about the Harrison family.

"What did he say?" He enunciated each word.

Talbert huffed. "Kept going on about how we couldn't use his real name. How he had to check in with someone, and if he didn't, they'd find out and things would get a whole lot worse." He scoffed. "Guy's obviously only worried about himself. Probably got a rich daddy somewhere who's going to cut off his trust fund if he gets busted again."

Jason squeezed the edge of the desk to keep himself from grabbing Talbert by the shirt. "Did he mention any names?"

"Nah. Kept rambling on about how he was going to die and it was going to be on us."

"Did he call his lawyer?"

"Nope."

"Did he call anyone?"

"He did, but it wasn't a lawyer."

Talbert was going to be the death of him. "How do you know?"

"'Cause as soon as he hung up he asked for another call so he could call the lawyer this time. Told him to forget it. Guy too stupid to use his call to get a lawyer can wait for the public defender."

"Do we have a name yet?"

"Nope. Still waiting on prints."

"Where is he now?"

"In interrogation. Waiting for you." Jason was halfway down the hall before Talbert finished talking. He grabbed his cell phone. Hit the redial button. "Kyle. Lock the place down."

There was a two-second pause before Kyle responded. "On it."

"I'll call you in a few." He didn't like Kyle, but he had to hand it to him. He didn't mess around with random questions when there wasn't time.

Michael stood outside the door. "What's wrong with you?"

Jason pointed to the door. "He called someone when he got here, but Talbert says it wasn't a lawyer. He also says he's been ranting about how he was going to be killed for this. We need to find out who he called and get some patrols out to Caroline's house. Now. He may have called someone to finish his job."

"Done." Michael sprinted away.

Jason made sure the recording equipment was on. No way he wanted this guy to get off on any sort of technicality.

He burst through the door. "What were you doing on the Harrison property tonight?"

The perpetrator scrambled out of his seat and came to a stop in a half crouch. What on earth? Had Jason scared him that much?

Frenzied eyes blinked at him. He saw him take in the badge. The notepad. Distrust emanated from every twitching muscle fiber.

Still in a defensive posture, he glared at Jason. "Who are you?"

Jason scraped the chair along the floor before he sat. Whoever this guy was scared of, he must believe they had the resources to infiltrate a detention center. Or that they were already part of the law enforcement community.

Jason studied him. The stage had lost a true artist if this guy was faking his fear.

He pointed to the chair across from him. "I'm Detective Jason Drake with the Henderson County Sheriff's Office. Why don't you have a seat and you can tell me who you are and why you were twenty feet up a tree on private property tonight."

One quick shake of the head was the only response.

"Fine. No name given, so I'm going to call you George. Makes it easier on me. You don't look like a George, but whatever."

He started writing on the legal pad he'd brought with him.

"I need protection."

"Excuse me? I didn't quite catch that."

"George" slid into the chair across from Jason and leaned across the table. His eyes,

though still frenzied, were now wide and imploring. "Please. They'll kill my kid."

Jason sat back in his chair. Was this guy
playing him? He didn't believe him, yet. But
whether it was true or not, he needed to hear
this story.

"Names."

"George" slid back in his seat. "No way.
You have no idea."

"I didn't mean your bosses' names."

"What?"

"*Your* name. Your kid's name. If you honestly believe your kid's in danger, you'd better start talking so we can get some protective
custody for...him? Her?"

"They'll know."

"If they're as powerful as you seem to think
they are, then you should assume they already
know you're in here. Start talking."

"Why should I trust you?"

The words were harsh, and the anguish in
"George's" eyes had Jason's hair standing up
on the back of his neck.

"I'm your only hope. Take it or leave it."

"George" dropped his face in his hands. "I have a son. And a wife. Well, I *had* a wife. We're divorced. She hates me, but I still love her. Our little boy has heart issues. Had a bunch of surgeries. Needs medicine. I had insurance, but even with that the debt kept growing. I started gambling. Got in too deep to the wrong people. Now they own me."

He looked up. "My boy's name is Mark. They know where he is. They'll kill him. Same as they'll kill that woman and the little boy. I don't know whose bad side she got on, but they won't stop until the kid is dead. I'm sorry. I really am."

Time to find out just how sorry. "How did you get into the house?"

"George" slumped in his chair. "From that tree stand you found me in tonight there's a clear line of sight to the keypad on the alarm system."

"You watched her punch in the code?"

"Yep. I've been in the house a couple of times to try it out."

"Did you mess with the water heater, too?"

"Yes."

"The fire ants?"

He shrugged. "I saw she had a lot of anti-histamines and EpiPens stashed everywhere. Took a chance that the bites might set off an allergic reaction. Not sorry it didn't work."

He wasn't sorry? Interesting. "Did you leave that picture for us to find?"

"George" didn't respond, but he didn't look surprised, either.

"Who hired you?"

"I don't know."

Jason slammed his hand on the table. "You told me they're going to kill your family. You know them well enough to know that much. Give me something."

"I need protection before I tell you anything else."

Jason shook his head. "You haven't given me enough to go on. You could be faking this whole thing to get set up somewhere with a new life. How do I know it's legitimate? You haven't even told me your name yet."

"Larry," he said. "Larry Sanders."

"Where are you from, Larry?"

"Greenville. North Carolina. Not South Carolina."

"I know where Greenville is."

Larry looked at him. Again with the pleading eyes. This guy was killing him. "I'm in debt. They paid off my kid's hospital bills, wiped out my gambling debts in full. But if I don't do the job…"

"What do you know about them?"

"I know this isn't the first time they've taken a hit out on somebody."

"Who?"

"Some guy in Wilmington."

Jason hoped his face didn't give anything away. "Wilmington?"

"Some kid in jail. Made it look like a jailbreak gone bad, but that was just a cover."

"Why did they want him dead?"

"No idea, but I'm guessing it's related to why they want the kid dead."

Jason tried to keep his breathing even. "Do you know the guy's name?"

"Nah. Just heard about it. Shouldn't be too hard to find in the papers."

Jason studied Larry. Larry studied his hands. Every facet of his body language showed defeat. The guy could be faking...but Jason doubted it. "Who did you call earlier?"

Larry's eyes flew to his face. "My wife. Told her to split. We had a plan."

"Where's she headed?"

Larry shook his head. "No way. Not until you offer me something. I've told you more than I should. You have enough to go on."

Jason stood. "I'm going to check out your story. If you've lied to me about anything, you'll get no help from me."

Larry shook his head, sorrow etching his face. "Don't take this the wrong way, but I'm past any help you can give me. If it's all the same to you, I'll be praying."

This guy was a study in contrasts. A criminal family man? A praying hit man?

Or a man willing to pretend to be anything in order to avoid jail?

"You keep praying. I'll do the same."

* * *

Caroline paced the floor of her living room. She'd made exactly seventeen passes when the sound of the door opening shattered her nerves. Her mind registered the face in front of her before her body did. "Where have you been?"

Kyle backed up a step. "Whoa. I've been gone less than three minutes. No need to start yelling. And put that thing down."

She lowered the weapon. "I didn't yell."

One eyebrow ticked up as he studied her. She hadn't *meant* to yell. He'd told her to grab her gun as he raced out the door. Did he really expect her to react to that *calmly*? She needed answers, and she needed them yesterday.

She made a conscious effort to speak in a softer tone. "Will you please tell me what's going on?"

"No idea."

"For crying out loud, Kyle."

He held up his hands again in mock surrender. "I don't. Okay?" He tapped his phone. "Your boyfriend called. Told me to lock the place down. He didn't elaborate and I didn't ask any questions. So until we hear back from him, or until the cavalry arrives, we're going to stay alert. Okay?"

"What part of that do you think is okay with me?"

She didn't know how much more of this she could take. Had it been only three nights ago that her biggest concern had been watching the latest episode of *Masterpiece Theatre* she'd recorded?

The most unusual aspect of her life at that moment was the child sleeping in the next room. Sure, it wasn't your typical everyday experience—adopting your dead best friend's son—but it was hardly dangerous.

At least, she hadn't expected it to be.

"Here they come," Kyle said from the dining room. He'd set up an array of laptops on the table. How many men traveled with six computers, at least three tablets and a few gadgets she didn't recognize?

"Who?"

"The cavalry."

A siren pierced the air. "Why are they doing that?"

"No need to be subtle. If there's someone else out there, someone thinking about trying to get to you tonight, there's no reason not to make a show of force."

That made sense.

She rubbed her temples. "I'm going to make some coffee."

Kyle nodded without looking away from the screen. "Probably a good idea. It's going to be a long night for those guys."

"For me, too."

He jumped up and blocked her path to the kitchen. "No. Not for you."

Was he crazy?

"If you think I'm going to bed—"

"That's exactly what I think."

"Not happening."

"Yes, it is."

"You can't make me go to bed, Kyle Richards. This is my life. My son's life. I can't afford—"

"What you can't afford is to be unable to

focus. This isn't going to be resolved tonight, and you're dead on your feet. I'd guess you are no more than ten minutes from a crash. The adrenaline you've been running on for the past hour will be gone and you'll be left with nothing to keep you going."

"Until the next attack sends my adrenaline through the roof again."

He put his hands on her upper arms. She resisted the urge to throw her arms back and try some of the self-defense moves Heidi had taught her. Kyle probably knew those moves, too—and how to parry them. Besides, fighting with him right now would be a waste of valuable energy.

"Listen to me," he said. His eyes burned with intensity, his face closer than she wanted it to be. "I will not let anyone touch you. Or Henry. I will wake you up at the first hint of danger. I will tell you about any news. But if you don't close your eyes for at least a couple of hours, you're going to put yourself into a deficit you can't recover from."

"You—"

"I'm trained for this. And I know where my limits are and what to do if I'm forced to exceed them. You don't, and this isn't the time to find out."

"But what if Jason—"

"Drake will be busy at the jail for the rest of the evening. If he needs you to identify anything or answer any questions, I will wake you up."

She disagreed with him on all fronts. But arguing seemed futile.

"Fine." She turned on her heel. "I expect a full report via text every hour."

Kyle huffed. "Yes, ma'am."

She stepped into her room and closed the door. As tempting as her bed was right now, she had no intention of stretching out on it. She had other plans.

She walked into her closet. It was huge. Too big. She'd designed it back when she spent more money on clothes each week than she now did on diapers. Over the years, her tastes—and her spending habits—had moderated.

In addition to her clothes, there was a lot of

room for other items, including the boxes that had come from Henry's nursery in Stephanie's house. She'd glanced through them in those early days. They contained a hodgepodge of framed photos, decorations, a baby book. Nothing that had been essential to her transition from single woman to single mom.

Maybe the answer to Henry's mysterious past was hidden in them.

Maybe it wasn't, but she wouldn't be able to sleep until she'd gone through everything she could get her hands on.

FOURTEEN

It was after midnight in North Carolina, but Jason had no way of knowing where Heidi was or what she was doing. He called the number she'd left for him and wasn't surprised when it went straight to voice mail. He left a brief message requesting that she contact him and ended the call.

He resisted the urge to rest his head on the cool metal of his desk. Instead, he slid the computer keyboard toward him. Time to find out if anyone had died in a Wilmington jail in the past couple of years.

He wasn't so arrogant as to believe that no one could fool him, but he trusted his internal lie detector. Larry might not know the details of the "accidental" jail death he'd referred to, but something told him digging deeper would give them some essential answers.

And maybe a few other things would start to make sense.

Had Stephanie been running for her life? And Henry's? What had she known?

And why hadn't she warned Caroline?

Jason clicked open good old Google. He could go through law enforcement databases to find what he needed, but right now he wasn't looking for the official account.

All he wanted was a name.

The search engine spit out more jail deaths than he'd anticipated. A few more clicks and he found what he was looking for.

Wilmington, NC—Officials thwarted an attempted jailbreak Tuesday morning. No officers were wounded. Three inmates suffered minor injuries. One inmate, Charles Townsend, thirty-two, died from injuries believed to have been sustained during his attempted escape.

Jason scanned the rest of the report.

Charles Townsend.

He punched the name into his computer. Moments later, he had an arrest record—and a mug shot.

He stared into the eyes of a man no older than himself. Eyes that he'd seen before.

Henry's eyes.

He wouldn't need the paternity testing to confirm it. This was what Henry would look like in thirty years.

He scanned through the report. Arrested on drug possession.

That was an easy enough thing to plant on someone innocent. Put some drugs in someone's car, then bust out a taillight or stage an accident to get the police to search the vehicle. Guy gets caught red-handed.

But why no bail? Surely Stephanie would have bailed him out.

He read on.

Oh boy.

His phone rang. "Drake."

"Detective Drake," the voice on the other end of the line spoke in a crisp tone.

"Special Agent Zimmerman."

She laughed. "It's Heidi. Whatcha got?"

He filled her in on everything that had happened. From his suspicion that there might be information in Stephanie's belongings at the Crawfords' house to his interrogation of Larry and his suspicions about Charles Townsend. She didn't interrupt. He appreciated that, but at one point he was afraid he was talking into thin air until the sound of fingers tapping across a keyboard filtered through the line.

"I have his mug shot," Heidi said at last. "The resemblance to Henry is uncanny." The typing continued. "Give me one second," she said.

He waited, his eyes continuing to study Charles Townsend. What had he gotten into? What had he been afraid of? Who was he? Because he doubted that Charles Townsend was his real name.

"Okay," Heidi said. "I'm headed to the coast."

"What?"

"I just got back to my office in DC. I would have been home this afternoon, but I've changed my flight plans. I'll do some digging about Charles Townsend here, and I'll go interview the sheriff in Wilmington."

Jason's head spun. "Okay."

"Look, I'm not trying to step on your toes, but I can be there in a few hours. It's an eight-hour drive for you. Plus you'd have to leave Caroline and Henry, and I'm sure you don't want to do that."

His skin flushed. How could she know?

"Truth is, I don't want you to, either. My husband and daughter will be home in about sixteen hours, and I'd rather you stay there and make sure they aren't returning to a war zone."

Jason couldn't argue with her logic.

"Let me do some legwork in Wilmington. Flashing a federal badge might help speed things along. You get to the Crawfords. Show up this morning and beg if you have to. We know so much more than we did yesterday— maybe it will be enough to convince them to help. There could be clues, a letter or a legal document, a photograph. Something that can help us tie all of this together."

"Yeah," he agreed. "Because until we figure out who is behind this, and why, we are chasing thin air."

"Exactly," she said. "You can get my regular cell phone number from Caroline. It will work now. Keep me informed. I'll do the same."

Jason printed all the info he'd uncovered on Charles Townsend. As it printed, his phone beeped.

A text from Heidi? Already? He stared at the words on the screen.

Your hunch was right. Charles Townsend = fake name. Got my best computer guy on it.

They were getting close. So close. But the realization brought no comfort.

The closer they got to finding out what was going on, the greater the danger Caroline and Henry were in.

The last sheet printed. He grabbed the pages and sprinted for the door.

"Where's the fire?" Michael called after him. He caught him on the stairs. "What's going on?"

Jason gave him the condensed version.

"What do you want me to do?"

Jason considered his options. "Stay put for now. I may need you here if we end up needing a warrant for the Crawfords' house. If Mr. Crawford lets us in, I'm going to want you to help us sort through Steph's stuff."

Michael nodded. "You got it."

Jason hit his lights and flew through the early morning stillness. He made one stop for coffee and pastries. Something told him this was a day that would require a lot of both.

When he cut the engine in Caroline's driveway, Kyle met him at the door. He took the coffee box and nodded. "Good call. We're going to need this."

"Have you talked to Heidi?" Jason assumed she would have called Caroline. Or Kyle. Or both.

"Yeah. She lit into Caroline for not sleeping. Lit into me for not making her. Then told us she'd already talked to you and you were bringing more info on Stephanie's husband before her phone started ringing and she had to go."

Caroline didn't sleep? After what he'd told her? "Where is she?" He could hear the growl in his words.

"In her room. Henry's still asleep."

Well, that was something to be thankful for.

He pulled out a cinnamon roll and tossed it on a paper plate. Maybe if he brought a peace offering, she wouldn't hate him.

Because he was about to give her a boulder-sized piece of his mind.

Caroline pulled another paper from the box. There had to be something useful in here. Something that would make it all clear. But she'd been at it for hours and had found only more dry, boring paperwork. So boring, in fact, that she'd dozed off a few times. Each time she'd awakened in a panic.

If Stephanie had tried to leave a clue, she'd done too good of a job hiding it.

"Caroline?"

The voice was familiar, but she jumped to her feet in surprise.

Jason.

Like a killer would have bothered to announce himself. She needed to get a grip.

Jason held her gaze. She didn't need him to say what he was thinking. She could read it on his face. He was not happy.

"I didn't go to bed."

"I noticed." He took a deep breath. Was he counting to ten in his head? He looked like he might start yelling at any moment. "You should have—"

She spoke fast. "It's not because I didn't think you were right. About needing sleep," she said. The thought of sleep elicited a yawn.

Jason shook his head several times, his aggravation obvious. Then he did the last thing she'd expected. He shrugged. "You can do whatever you want, Caroline."

Oh no. This was worse than the argument

she'd been bracing for. She'd rather deal with his frustration than his apathy.

He put a cinnamon roll on her dresser, and she could tell he was struggling to keep his tone civil. "I stopped for coffee. Whenever you're done here, we need to talk."

He turned on his heel and marched out of her room.

Well, that was just great. He wasn't the one people were trying to kill. If she wanted to stay up all night looking for clues, that was her prerogative.

So why did she feel like she'd been caught with her finger in the icing?

If she'd found something—anything—he wouldn't be mad. Well, he might still be mad, but he would have gotten over it.

She reached for the little teddy bear in the bottom of the box, wondering how it had gotten mixed up in a box of paperwork. She thought the toys had all been packed together. Maybe this one hadn't been in the toy chest for some reason? It was cute, plush with a sweet navy ribbon around his neck. She fingered the bow, noticing it was skewed.

It was ridiculous, but at least this was one thing she could fix. She had a real knack for tying bows.

Good grief. Someone had knotted this poor rib—

Her hands trembled.

Get a grip, Caroline. It's just a knot. But…

She wasn't imagining it. There was something stuck in the ribbon. She worked the knot as carefully as she could. The ribbon had been wrapped multiple times around something small. It wouldn't be obvious to anyone who wasn't messing with the bow.

A few more loops untangled.

A ring dropped into her hand.

A ring with a family crest.

"Jason!"

She was annoyed with him, but her first impulse had been to call him.

He ran into her room. "What is it?"

Apparently his first impulse was to run to her.

Something about that made her yearn to run straight into his arms, but she forced herself to remain where she was.

"Caroline?"

Hoping he'd believe her agitation was due to the ring, and not to the way he was making her emotions ping around in her heart, she held up her discovery. "I have no idea what this is, but I'm sure it's important."

He reached for the ring. She expected him to take it from her, but his hand rested beneath hers and wrapped around it. She looked into his eyes.

"I'm sorry," he said. "It's your life, and I know you believe you have the most to lose."

She should say something witty, but all she could do was nod.

"I was angry because I'm worried about you. And when I'm worried, I tend to overreact."

"I remember."

"Some things never change," he said with a shrug.

"Some things do. You apologized."

He smirked. "True." He looked like he wanted to say something else. She saw the moment he decided against it. "May I?"

She nodded, and he lifted the ring from her hand. He studied it. "What do you make of it?"

"It's a family crest. That kind of ring used to be pretty common with certain wealthy families. Usually families that have old money." She knew Jason had major issues with people who inherited their money. He'd always made an exception for her and Blake. Said that they weren't spoiled. She knew where his negative feelings about money came from. His biological father had a lot of money he'd inherited. "A ring like this," she said, "would typically be passed down from father to son. Maybe to a grandson."

"Firstborn?" Jason continued to study the ring.

"Usually, but not necessarily."

"Do the items on the crest mean anything to you?"

"No. We don't have one, and I never got into that kind of thing."

"Where did you find it?" She showed him how it had been tied into the bow of the teddy bear. His eyes grew large. "That was Stephanie's way of hiding something for you to find? You could have tossed that bear in the trash or donated it."

"True."

"What made you look?"

"The bow wasn't even."

"The bow—" He laughed. Then laughed harder. "Now I get it."

Kyle poked his head in the door, Henry in his arms. "Care to let me in on the joke?"

"No joke," Jason said. "But Caroline is the only one who's going to be able to uncover any of Stephanie's clues." He showed Kyle the ring. "She hid this one on a teddy bear."

Caroline tuned them out as they had a good laugh at her expense. So what if she couldn't leave a picture crooked on the wall? Or a bow with uneven tails? That didn't mean she was a nutcase.

She scrambled to her feet and reached for Henry. She pulled off a piece of the cinnamon roll, and Henry opened his mouth like a baby bird. "Let's get some breakfast and catch up." She glanced at Jason. "I'm guessing you have news for me."

Jason continued to study the ring. "Between my news and this ring, we may be close to finding out who Henry's dad is."

FIFTEEN

Caroline settled Henry into his high chair. She traced his nose, lips and chin with her fingertip. He grinned at her. The grin that sometime over the past year had become the one he reserved for her and her alone. The grin that said "You're my mommy and I think you're awesome."

Her stomach clenched as she rested her palm against his cheek. How could anyone want to harm him? Why? What could she do to stop them?

What if she failed?

"Hey," Jason said from behind her. "You okay?"

Was she okay? "I don't know."

He moved toward her, then stopped. Why had he stopped?

"Let's compare notes and see how you feel then."

They scooted Kyle's assortment of laptops to one side of the table and sat. Well, she sat. Kyle paced from one computer to the next, eyes scanning the screens. She had no idea what he was looking for, and she no longer had the mental energy to ask. Jason leaned against the buffet she'd inherited from her grandmother.

"You first," she said.

A self-satisfied grin crossed his features as he handed her a sheet of paper from the folder he'd been carrying. "Look familiar?"

She studied the mug shot. This picture was of a man, probably in his early thirties, with dark blond hair and...

She looked at Jason. "Who is this?"

"I don't know, yet."

"Who do you think he is?" she asked.

"Who do *you* think he is?"

Fear coursed through her at his words. The wavy hair, the shape of the nose and forehead, those eyes. She'd never been any good at the "he looks like his father" or "she's the spitting image of her grandmother" game. But you'd have to have zero observational skills to miss this connection. Was this man…? No. Stephanie said Henry's father had died. But what if he was a living relative—maybe a brother?

She couldn't find her voice.

Kyle could. "Looks like a grown-up version of Henry. Is that the little guy's dad?"

Jason explained what he knew.

"So, this guy was killed in a jail riot while Stephanie was pregnant with Henry. And the charges could have been trumped up. And the guy you arrested last night says the same people who are trying to kill Henry had this guy killed?" Kyle asked.

Jason nodded. "Accurate summary."

"Well, what's his name? What else do we know about him?"

Jason's earlier confidence vanished. "Not much. The name he was arrested under is fake."

"Fake?"

"Good enough to stand up under the initial

court proceedings that landed him in jail. But it only took Heidi about ten minutes to figure out it wasn't real."

"Heidi?" Caroline asked.

"Yes. She was in DC when we spoke earlier. She was headed to Wilmington this morning to do some snooping around. I'm hoping we'll have some info from her soon."

"What kind of snooping around?"

Kyle snorted. "The kind she does best."

"Which is?"

He grinned at her. "Heidi can be very persuasive. My guess is she'll start out sweet. And if she doesn't get the answers she wants when she wants them, she'll go spicy on them fast."

Caroline looked at Jason, then back at Kyle. "That is not an answer. I've seen Heidi's spicy side. What, specifically, will she do?"

There was so much in this situation that was out of her control. But she felt she at least had the right to be told what information they had. She would not sit back while everyone made decisions on her behalf and she would not be kept in the dark. It was her life. And Henry's. If she lost Henry now… No. She would not go there.

Jason pulled out a chair and sat at the end of the table. "Heidi didn't explain her plan. However, if I had gone to Wilmington today, I would have started at the police station. I would have explained—very politely—that I was looking into the death of an inmate while making sure not to antagonize the local law enforcement officers or make them feel like I was trying to step on their toes."

"What would you be hoping to achieve from this conversation?"

"More details. The inside story about what happened as opposed to the sanitized version that was undoubtedly all the press heard. Was there an investigation? Were there corrupt officers involved? Had there been any clue that Charles Townsend wasn't his real name or that he was hiding something?"

"Would they tell you all that?"

"Maybe, maybe not. But I wouldn't just pay attention to what they'd say."

Caroline handed Henry another piece of the cinnamon roll. "What else is there?"

"Body language can be very revealing. Sometimes you get no answers to your questions, but you find out who knows more than they're sharing, or which clerk might be willing to talk to you later. That kind of thing. Sometimes you go in and ask questions knowing full well you won't get answers. Then you step back and watch to see what reaction your questions stir up."

Kyle banged his coffee cup on the table. "Kick the hive."

Kicking the hive was an analogy she could follow. "Then what?"

"That's when it gets fun. You follow people around. You make phone calls. You talk to more people. Eventually you find the person who wants the truth to come out."

"Or somebody shoots you," Kyle muttered.

"Helpful," Jason said. Jason was fluent in sarcasm, and Kyle definitely brought it out in him.

"I don't need the kiddie version, Jason. And,

Kyle, I doubt anyone is going to shoot Heidi." The squabbling between these two was going to make her crazy.

"So the bottom line is, Heidi is going to try to find out who Charles Townsend really was?"

"Yes."

"And what are we going to do?"

"First, we are going to do some research on this crest."

Kyle rubbed the stubble on his chin. "I can help with that. Should be able to sniff around a few databases."

Jason agreed. He didn't look happy about it, but he agreed.

"What else do we need to do?" she asked.

"We need to get cleaned up and go ask Mr. Crawford to let us look through Stephanie's stuff."

Ugh. Again with Stephanie's stuff. "Fine."

Jason checked his watch. Ten thirty. Mrs. Crawford should be at church and then headed out to lunch.

Caroline set Henry's diaper bag on the hood of the car. "Are you sure about this?"

"No," Jason admitted. "But now that we know Stephanie deliberately hid at least one clue, we need to go through her things."

Caroline rested her head on the door frame. "I don't want to fight with them."

"We won't." She didn't look convinced. "We'll be respectful. We'll explain that we have new information, and we'll hope Mrs. Crawford stays gone long enough for us to get what we need."

Caroline strapped Henry into his car seat and put her own seat belt on without further comment. Was she still mad at him? Did she disagree with this step in the investigation?

He put the Explorer in Drive. "Hello?" He bumped her arm with his.

She looked at him like she was trying to memorize his features for a lineup or something. Did he have cinnamon on his lips? Because she was definitely looking at his lips.

Her face flushed, and her eyes dropped to her hands. "Let's get this over with. I can't believe I'm missing church to go badger a grieving father about his dead daughter's belongings. I feel dirty doing this."

He reached for her hand before he could stop himself. He should keep both hands on the wheel. But her hand slid into his, and it fit so right.

"I promise I'll be nice."

"You'd better be."

They rode mostly in silence, and when they arrived, Jason parked the Explorer behind Mr. Crawford's old truck. Jason hopped to the ground, planning to make a beeline for the other side of the car to open Caroline's door.

But...something wasn't right. Mr. Crawford's truck door was open. So was the front door. He reached back in and grabbed her arm. "Slide into the driver's seat."

Her eyes widened, but she didn't argue. She moved across the console, her purse in her hand. "Is your gun in there?" he asked.

She nodded.

"Good. Keep the car running. Turn it around so you don't have to back out of the driveway if you have to leave in a hurry. And if I tell you to go, floor it."

As soon as he edged away from the car, he heard her throw it in Reverse.

Then he heard another sound.

A grown man. Sobbing.

He raced toward the house.

"Mr. Crawford! Mr. Crawford!" He ran through the open doorway and paused on the landing of the split-level.

"How could this have happened?" Mr. Crawford's heartbroken voice came from the lower level. Jason bolted down the stairs.

"Mr. Crawford, are you okay?"

He found Mr. Crawford standing in a foot of water at the bottom of the stairs, tears etching his face. "Do I look okay to you, son?"

Jason tried to grasp the magnitude of the devastation. The walls of this room were lined with boxes. There was no question that the contents of the bottom row of boxes would be ruined. But the great tragedy was the canvases floating across the room.

At least twenty of Stephanie's paintings now

bobbed in the water. Ten of the larger works still leaned against the boxes, their weight holding them in place while the bottom foot of each canvas was submerged. Could they be salvaged? Restored? Jason honestly had no idea.

He'd deal with that later. He ran to the bedroom. He checked the closet, then the bathroom, then the garage.

Clear. He started to go upstairs to check the main living areas.

"Don't bother. I already looked. There's no one else here," Mr. Crawford said. "Me and the missus went to the early service at church. She likes to stay for a ladies Sunday school class sometimes, and then they all go to lunch and gossip. I stopped over at the flea market before I came home. Walked in to find all this. I cut the water off at the main. Thought a pipe had burst somehow, but it was the bathtub. The plug was in. The water was on. It overflowed," Mr. Crawford said. His words pulled forth another sob. "We never use that bathroom," he said. "Can't remember the last time that tub was used. How you reckon it got plugged and the water turned on? It sure wasn't me or the missus."

Jason wanted to look away. Had he ever seen a grown man so shattered? Mr. Crawford probably didn't want his sympathy, but he couldn't stand here without addressing his pain.

"I am so very sorry." He put one hand on his shoulder. "Mr. Crawford, Caroline and Henry are in the car. Let me go explain what's going on and I'll be right back."

A barely perceptible nod was the only response. It would have to do.

Jason took the stairs two at a time. Caroline had done as he asked. When she saw him, she threw open the passenger door.

"It's okay," he said. Well, it wasn't. "Put it in Park. We need to talk."

He walked to the driver's side and explained what had happened.

"You don't think it was an accident? Could they have forgotten…?"

"Not a chance."

"But if someone did this deliberately, how could they have known we were coming here to look through Stephanie's things today? Kyle swept my house for bugs. And they haven't messed with Stephanie's family or her belongings before."

"It could be a coincidence...but that doesn't seem likely."

"What do we do now?"

"I'll call the guys and help Mr. Crawford reach his insurance agent. They have companies that specialize in this kind of thing. Drying stuff out, restoring art."

"Stephanie's paintings?"

"All wet. Some of them might be salvageable."

Caroline blinked back tears. "I have a couple of her pieces at the house, in Henry's room," she said.

"Caroline, Henry can't be downstairs. Everything is wet. There's no place to put him down, and I don't want him out of our sight," he said.

"I'll hold him," she said. Her chin jutting out, her mouth in a line. "I want to see it."

"Fine. Let me call Kyle first. He needs to figure out how they knew we were coming."

He stepped away from the car, scanning the driveway and the woods around the house. Could Kyle be trusted? He hadn't trusted the FBI agent at first, but he had to admit that was mostly because of the way Kyle looked at Caroline. Like he had a special relationship with her. Like he wanted it to be more than it was.

But now? He needed to be able to trust Kyle. And he wasn't sure he could count on his own judgment to be impartial.

He called Heidi.

She answered on the first ring, and he filled her in. "I need to know how much you trust Kyle," he said. "He swept the house and said there were no listening devices, but this happens an hour before we show up to go through Stephanie's things," he said. "If they know about the ring..."

"I trust him with my life," she said with no hesitation. "I appreciate your questioning it.

It's a valid concern." He had to give it to her; she wasn't dismissing his worries based on her history with Kyle alone. "But we're dealing with a sophisticated enemy. Talk to Kyle. Have him recheck the house, the car, everything."

Jason looked back at the car, where Caroline now stood with Henry, the diaper bag over her shoulder.

The diaper bag.

It couldn't be.

"I have an idea of how they may be listening," he said, walking farther away from Caroline. "But that's not the most important thing. If they know where we are, we're sitting ducks. I need to get some backup over here."

"Agreed. Call me back when things are secure."

He called in a request for backup to the Crawfords' residence. Then called Kyle.

"I think there might be a bug in the diaper bag," he said.

"What?"

"Have you checked the diaper bag for bugs?"

Kyle huffed. "The scanner would have—"

"Even if the diaper bag was in the car?"

"What?"

"She's been leaving it in the car a lot."

Kyle muttered something under his breath. "I'll be there in fifteen minutes," Kyle said. "I'll check the car, the diaper bag, the car seat, your clothes, Caroline's clothes, Henry's pacifier, everything."

Jason pulled out the notepad he kept in his pocket and wrote a few quick lines.

The diaper bag might be bugged. Leave it in the car.

When he showed Caroline the note, her eyes popped wide, but she gave no other reaction. She removed the bag from her shoulder and returned it to the backseat of the car.

She gave him a weak smile. "Let's go see if we can help Mr. Crawford."

He reached for Henry. "May I?" Henry lunged for him, and Caroline handed him over with no argument.

"Thanks. He's getting heavy." She massaged her arm and then leaned closer to him. "How bad is it?"

"It's bad. My guess is most of her things are ruined."

Caroline gulped and blew out a long breath. "Okay," she said, squaring her shoulders. "I'm ready."

SIXTEEN

She hadn't been ready.

Not for the devastation. Not for Mr. Crawford's tearful hug. Not for her own sense of loss.

Not for the guys from the sheriff's office and local fire department who showed up with shop vacs and squeegees and who pumped out the downstairs and carried soggy boxes outside.

Not for Papa and Mama Drake to materialize in the driveway with snacks and toys and a pack 'n' play for Henry.

She hadn't been ready for Kyle to scan her, Henry, her purse, Henry's car seat and the diaper bag, and for him to point to the diaper bag as the culprit.

The stupid diaper bag.

Someone had been close enough to her and to Henry to bug the diaper bag? When? How?

Who?

Why?

She tried to remember what they'd talked about when the diaper bag had been around. Did they—the mysterious and unidentified they—know about the ring?

Henry chattered happily from his spot on the porch. As the guys brought the water-logged boxes out, she went through them.

She had no idea what she was looking for. She found Stephanie's journals, but she was afraid to open them. Most of the pages were stuck together, and when she tried to separate them, they tore and the ink smeared.

There might be an answer hidden there, but it would remain hidden for now. Maybe she could look again when the pages had dried out a little.

She looked at the canvases that now rested all along the porch floor. There'd been an intense debate about how to try to salvage them.

For now, they had them lying horizontally and they had touched them as little as possible.

The oils had held up okay, although the canvases would have to be restretched over new frames. But the watercolors had bled into swirls. One that she knew had been of the ocean now resembled something Henry might do with finger paints.

Someone brought sub sandwiches. When this was over, she might never eat a sub sandwich again.

Mrs. Crawford returned home and her anguish at the loss had been borne by Mr. Crawford, but they could all hear her cries. When the worst was over, Mama Drake had brought her a glass of tea and a slice of banana bread and now sat with her on the porch.

The guys took turns playing with Henry, who was having the time of his life. He was walked all over his grandparents' property. He got wagon rides and long swings on the porch swing with Papa Drake, and Caroline kept looking.

"How's it going?" She didn't look up. Jason

had checked on her every fifteen minutes. It was almost annoying.

Almost.

"I don't know. Looking for a needle that may or may not exist? How do you ever know if you're done?"

She pulled the lid off another box, and the sides gave way. Stuffed animals from Stephanie's childhood spilled to the floor.

"Hey." Jason knelt beside her, one hand resting on her knee. "You're doing great. And you're doing all you can do. No one can ask more of you, Caroline."

She looked into his face. What would she do when he disappeared from her life again? She pulled a small metal box out of the stuffed animals. She opened it and found an assortment of paintbrushes and markers.

"What is it?" Jason asked.

"I remember this box," she said. "Stephanie carried it all through elementary school. Some of these pens wrote in invisible ink. And one of them had a secret compartment. We used to pretend we were spies..."

She picked up the pen.

Could it be?

She pulled off the end and turned it upside down.

A mini SD card fell into her hand. As small as a fingernail. Still dry.

"I'm guessing you guys didn't hide stuff on mini SD cards in elementary school," Jason said, reaching for the tiny chip.

"No."

"We may have found the needle."

Caroline stared at it. If Stephanie were standing here, she would strangle her. Could she have made it any harder?

The ring in the teddy bear's ribbon. The SD card in the box with all the other stuffed animals, in the pen that Caroline would recognize as a hiding place. That would have made sense to Stephanie. She probably thought it would be obvious. Or more likely, she thought she was hiding things no one would ever really need to find.

Kyle emerged with a laptop and a card

reader and an adapter to plug the SD card into the USB port of the laptop.

Who kept something like that on them? "Were you a Boy Scout?"

"Eagle Scout." He nodded toward the laptop. "This is what I do, Caroline. Now let's see what this baby tells us."

While he loaded the disk into the computer, Caroline asked, "Have you been able to find anything on the crest?"

He frowned at the screen. "No. I think it may be a proof."

Jason seemed to like that statement, but it didn't make any sense to her.

"A proof?"

"Like in the Bible when Tamar tricked Judah. The person who owned this is the man. That kind of thing. The ring has several very unique features. The crest may not be that unusual, but there are some old markings on the band that would be hard to fake or replicate. It would be difficult to backtrack the ring to the owner, but if we find out who Henry's dad was, that ring may be the proof."

"Seems like a paternity test would be a little more conclusive."

"It would," Jason agreed. "But the ring may make the family more willing to cooperate."

Caroline's mouth went dry. "The family?"

Henry had a family out there somewhere. She'd always known this. His father didn't exist in a vacuum. He didn't appear out of thin air. He had parents, maybe siblings. Maybe even other children. People who might be very interested in Henry.

But Stephanie hadn't wanted them involved in Henry's life. And here she was, hunting them down as if their lives depended on it.

Which they did.

"Here we go," Kyle said. He turned the screen to Caroline. "Seems like you should read it first."

"Thanks."

She adjusted the monitor. A basic word processing document filled the screen.

She read.

Lee told me never to write it down. But tonight, I feel compelled to share the story. Just in case something ever happens to me. More than likely this file will wind up in a landfill somewhere when my kids toss all my old stuff after I die. So be it.

I loved Lee so much. He swept me off my feet, and even after everything that happened, I have no regrets.

I don't know the full story. I know that he was born out of wedlock. His mother adored him and didn't tell him who his birth father was until she was dying. Finally she admitted she'd fallen in love with a married man. When she found out she was pregnant, she never thought twice about whether or not she would keep him.

Lee's father knew about him, but he'd returned to his wife and family, and Lee's mom never had any contact with him. Still, every now and then some money would be deposited into her checking account. Sometimes as much as several thousand dollars. She suspected it was

Lee's father. She never saw it as bribery to keep silent. She still loved him and had no desire to ruin him. She saw it as his attempt to help take care of his son.

She saved every dime of it and used it to pay for his college education.

Lee's father's wife passed away six years ago. After her death, he approached Lee's mom and asked about meeting Lee. She refused. He told her he respected her decision, but that he intended to put Lee in his will, and she should at least let Lee know so it wouldn't be a complete shock upon his death.

The night he told me this story, he confessed over the years he'd suspected that he was being watched from time to time. He wanted to believe it was his father, keeping an eye on him. But he also feared it might be his half brother, scheming to make sure Lee's existence didn't come to light.

A few nights before he was arrested, he told me he'd been certain someone was watching him as he drove to work. He was worried. We'd just found out I was pregnant, and he was afraid for me and the baby. He begged me to go home for a month or so while he figured out what was going on.

I was heartbroken. If it hadn't been for Henry, I would have refused. But I decided I could visit Mom and Dad for a week.

Two days later, he called me from jail. He'd been arrested. Broken taillight and drugs in his car. He'd never even smoked a cigarette, much less a joint. He told me they kept calling him Charles. That they had a driver's license with his picture but not his name. He told me he didn't know what was going on, but to stay away.

Then I saw in the news that he'd been killed in jail. I panicked. I know I should have told someone that I suspected he'd been killed deliberately. But I didn't.

I knew his main concern would have been that I protect Henry. My prayer is that someday there will be justice for Lee. If you are reading this, the man you want to talk to is Frederick Larrabie Jr. He's from Raleigh. He's Henry's grandfather. He shouldn't be too hard to find. He's one of the richest men in the country.

Caroline leaned back in her chair.

"It's the money. He's the heir to a fortune." She looked at Jason. "And somebody doesn't want him to have it."

Jason stared at the screen. Freddie Larrabie? His palms twitched as he considered the implications. He wanted to tell Caroline she was wrong, but he had a bad feeling that Caroline was dead-on. Someone had figured out that Lee was the illegitimate son of Frederick Larrabie. And they knew about Henry.

But there was no way Frederick Larrabie was involved in the attacks. *Please don't let him be involved in this.*

"Now what?" Caroline glared at the computer, then at him and Kyle. "I'll tell you one thing. Nobody had better suggest we meet with these people. They are not getting Henry. Not a chance."

"I need to make a phone call," Jason blurted out.

Caroline narrowed her eyes at him. "Now?"

"Now."

"Who do you need to call?"

Jason couldn't believe he was saying this. "My father."

He didn't hang around to talk to her about it. He didn't give himself time to talk himself out of it. He walked into the yard and dialed the number.

"Jason?" His father didn't hide his delight. "I'm glad you called."

Jason fought to keep his tone polite and respectful. He needed information. "I'm calling on official business, sir."

"Okay." A trace of disappointment lingered in the word. "How can I help?"

"I need to know everything you know about Frederick Larrabie. Particularly about his family."

"Freddie? Why?"

"I...can't get into it right now."

He waited. His father had played golf with Freddie Larrabie for the past twenty years. He knew his dad had gone on several business trips with the man—mainly because his father never missed an opportunity to brag about it.

"Okay. Want to meet for supper?"

Jason gulped. He'd known his father would do this—agree to help only in exchange for something he wanted. It was always this way. But this was not the time to fight with his birth father.

He glanced back at Caroline. He'd do it for her. He'd do anything for her. Even have supper with his birth father. "Where?"

"How about Hot Dog World. In an hour?"

At least he'd get a decent meal out of it. "Okay. See you there."

He slid the phone into his pocket. Caroline's hand on his arm startled him.

"Why did you call your father?" Caroline never referred to his birth father as his dad. She'd always respected the distinction.

"He knows Freddie Larrabie."

Her breath caught. "How do you know?"

Fair question. He'd spent most of his child-hood, and adulthood for that matter, trying to stay as far out of his father's business as possible.

"My father is a name-dropper. Freddie Lar-rabie is a big name to drop."

Caroline didn't say anything. "Do you think he'll help us?"

Us again.

"I don't know," he said. "But I have to try."

"Are they close?"

"I'm about to find out."

"Couldn't you talk about it on the phone? Why do you have to meet him in person?"

"His idea."

She studied his face. He saw the awareness in her eyes. He could pretend following a clue, even if it led to his father, was part of the in-vestigative process he would go through for any citizen, but she knew he was doing this for her.

"Do you want me to go with you?" she asked.

"Why? You don't like him, either."

"I don't want you to have to do it alone."

It was so tempting. His father would be more inclined to behave if Caroline was there. But he hated the idea of using her as a shield. "I'm a big boy. I can survive a meal with the man." Maybe.

She looked down. "I don't want…" She said more, but he couldn't catch it.

"What?"

Her face and neck were pink as she faced him. Was she embarrassed? Why?

"I said I don't want you to leave me." She ducked her head.

"Afraid I won't come back?" He deserved it if she was.

"No."

"Then what?"

"I just… don't…" She shook her head.

He pulled her toward him. He'd release her if she resisted him at all, but she didn't.

"Are you scared?" He whispered the words against her hair.

"Terrified."

"I would never leave you if I didn't think you'd be safe." She didn't respond. "But if you want, you and Henry can come with me."

"Thank you."

"No problem."

They should go inside. Kyle was probably watching them from a computer monitor. And the longer he held her, the harder it was to resist tilting her chin and claiming her lips again.

He stepped back. She laced her arm through his as they walked back to the house. "I don't promise to be nice to him," she warned him.

He patted her hand. "Sure."

She would be. She couldn't help it. She was nice to everyone.

SEVENTEEN

Forty-five minutes later, they parked in the Hot Dog World parking lot. Caroline grinned. "I love this place."

"This might ruin it for you forever."

"No chance," she said. "I'm hopelessly devoted to the onion rings."

"Stay close," he said.

"At least we're bug-free," she said, patting the grocery bag she'd thrown Henry's change of clothes into.

"Maybe you'll start a new trend with that thing," he said with a laugh.

The laughter died in his throat when he spotted his father at the door. Suit, tie, spit-shined shoes. Trim. Still had a head full of hair. Oozed confidence. He looked exactly the same as Jason remembered from all his worst childhood memories.

Maybe bringing Caroline had been a bad idea. He didn't want her to see how hard it was for him to be around this man.

"Mr. Slater." She extended her hand, the picture of grace and Southern charm. "Thank you for meeting with us."

There was that "us" again.

"Caroline." His father seemed genuinely pleased to see her. "This is a pleasant surprise. I haven't seen you since the Christmas party at the Fultons'. How are you? And how is this little guy?"

She laughed, and it sounded so natural. "Henry's great. Thank you for asking." She glanced at Jason. The look on her face was clear. It was time for him to play nice, too.

"Thank you for meeting us," he said. His version sounded stilted to his own ears, but his father accepted it.

"Happy to help. Let's order and you can ask me whatever you need."

They made it through the line, filled their

drinks, and then Caroline slid into a booth and settled Henry beside her. He squeezed in beside Henry. It was tight, but he couldn't blame her for wanting to keep Henry close. And he didn't mind being forced to sit so close to her. His father took the other side of the booth.

Henry kept all of them entertained while they made small talk as they waited on their food. When it arrived, Caroline flashed him a smile. "Jason, would you bless the food for us?"

"Of course," he said before offering the shortest grace possible.

"Now," his father said as he picked up an onion ring, "what on earth have you two gotten into now?"

"Sir?" Caroline was all innocence and confusion.

He shook his head. "Jason calls me out of the blue wanting info about Freddie Larrabie? And you show up with him? And with Henry? You couldn't have me more confused or curious if you tried."

Jason took a sip of his Coke. "How well do you know Freddie Larrabie, sir?"

His father leaned back in the booth. "I knew him over twenty years. No, make that thirty years. We used to play golf whenever I was in Raleigh." He looked between him and Caroline. "Why?"

"Knew him?"

"Yes. Freddie passed away about two years ago."

"How did he die?"

"Cancer. Pancreatic. Went pretty fast."

Jason looked at Caroline, and he could see his own confusion in her face. He'd been assuming Freddie Larrabie was alive and well.

"What can you tell us about him?"

His father dunked an onion ring in ketchup and took a bite before he answered. "He was a good guy and an excellent businessman. His son isn't as solid as he was, but he's turned into a decent CEO of the company. His grandkids, however, are some of the most spoiled and self-absorbed people I've ever had the misfortune to encounter."

He looked at Caroline, an appreciative smile on his face. "You and your brother, you two break the mold," he said. He took a drink and then gestured toward Caroline with his cup. "I run with a lot of wealthy families."

Here we go. More name-dropping.

"I'm sorry to say that often the older generations, the ones who worked hard and made the greatest sacrifices, somehow don't pass their integrity down. The kids get the money but not the work ethic. You and that brother of yours haven't let your money go to your heads," he said. "It's commendable. And rare." He turned his attention back to Jason. "If something's going on with the Larrabies, I'd suspect that bratty set of twin grandkids— Liam and Fern—are at the root of it. I suffered through a round of golf with the boy a few years ago, right before Freddie got sick."

He looked like he'd gotten a whiff of something rotten. "He spent the entire front nine trying to talk Freddie into buying him a new drone. Apparently it was his favorite hobby and he'd crashed his best one. It was like being around a five-year-old begging for a toy for Christmas."

Jason grabbed a notebook from his jacket pocket and wrote down the grandchildren's names. "Before we go any further, I need to know something. Can we speak to you about Larrabie with complete confidence?"

"Of course, son. I will help you, and Caroline, in any way I can."

Jason studied him. His dad was a lawyer. Some people would say he was a professional liar. But he didn't have time to argue.

"Fine." He laid out the facts as they knew them. His father listened, nodded his head in the appropriate places and didn't interrupt.

"This afternoon, we found a letter where Stephanie claimed that her husband, Henry's father, was the illegitimate son of none other than Frederick Larrabie."

That made his father put down his hot dog. "Wow."

An accurate summation.

His father cleared his throat. "I won't say this is a total surprise. Freddie was no saint.

But I would have thought he would be the kind of man who would take full responsibility for his actions."

Jason explained what Stephanie had shared in her letter.

"Sounds like he was trying to do the right thing, or at least that he was making some effort to be fair to his son." He leaned his head back in the booth. "So what's the motive for someone to come after Henry now?" He said it to himself, not looking for an answer. Jason met Caroline's gaze. She gave him an encouraging smile.

After a few more moments of internal debate, his father looked at both of them. "It has to be either the son, William, or the grandchildren, Liam and Fern. My guess is the grandchildren have the most to lose."

"What do you mean?"

"William Larrabie is only ten years younger than I am. He has his own money, and I've never seen any signs that he overspends or might have any debt issues. Whatever he inherited from Freddie would probably go straight into investments and then eventually to his children. He doesn't need that money for his day-to-day life, and it's unlikely he'd been counting on it for anything."

"So the grandkids…"

"Well, that's a whole different ball game," he said. "Last time I saw William, about a year ago, he complained that his kids had no interest in running the family business. He said they were more interested in living off their trust funds than doing anything productive with their lives."

Jason tried to picture it. "So their grandfather dies, they find out there's a secret son who might get a piece of the inheritance—if an investigator can track him down—and decide the best thing to do is get there first and get rid of him? Seems pretty drastic."

"That's why I'm wondering about the motive. It's one thing to be angry about someone taking half your inheritance, but to hunt him down, stage a crime, have him incarcerated and then killed? And then to later try to eliminate his son? That requires some serious determination and motivation, and I'm just not seeing it. I could call William and do a little fishing."

Caroline's face paled. "Mr. Slater, Stephanie was terrified of them. She wanted to be sure they never knew about Henry."

"Looks to me like they already do."

Caroline's stomach flipped at Mr. Slater's observation. He was right, but somehow having the words out there made it harder for her to pretend they were going to be able to get out of this without making contact with the Larrabie family.

Jason didn't seem convinced. "We have no proof of that. Everything we have is circumstantial. Stephanie pointed the finger and said they are dangerous. Unfortunately, we can't arrest anyone on that."

"You need to talk to William," his father said.

"And play right into their hands?"

"I'm not sure how talking to William is dangerous. From what you've told me, Freddie changed the will. If he did, then William already knows about Lee."

Caroline looked at Henry. Would they try to take him from her?

Mr. Slater patted her hand. "Caroline?" Her face heated as she realized she'd missed something. Mr. Slater's smile was kind, his eyes full of compassion. He bore little resemblance to her memory of the man who'd been the very real stuff of nightmares for Jason and Mama Drake. "I get your fear, but from what you've told me, Stephanie's trust documents were written specifically to ensure they would have no claim on her son. The reality is that all of us are human. We all fail. And some of us, myself included, royally messed up our lives when we were younger. We can't change our past mistakes, but I can tell you we wish we could and we'd give anything to make amends."

His eyes didn't leave her face as he spoke, but she knew he wasn't speaking to her anymore. In her peripheral vision, she saw Jason stiffen.

Mr. Slater leaned forward. "I have a friend who is a crackerjack estate lawyer. He could glance over Stephanie's paperwork to make sure it's solid if it would make you feel better. But if you think about this logically, rather than from a place of fear, I think you'll see no one would have any interest in removing Henry from your custody. William's in his fifties now, and I'm confident he has no interest in raising a toddler. And there's not a court in the land that would give custody to Liam or Fern."

His assurances made sense. Part of her fear of Henry's birth father's family was that there would be a sister or grieving mother of Stephanie's husband who would try to take him. But if the Larrabies were the family, there wasn't anyone who should have an interest in taking her son from her.

Mr. Slater smiled at her. "I'm sure it's hard for you to imagine what it's like to look in the mirror every day and know your life is a mess because of your own poor decisions." He glanced at Jason, who was now sitting at attention, jaw clenched. "Since you won't normally answer my calls, I'm going to go ahead and say what I've been trying to say to you for the past six months."

Jason put his hand up, but Mr. Slater pressed on. "I'm sorry."

Caroline wanted to crawl under the booth. She should not be here for this. But Jason's father wasn't paying any attention to her.

"I know you'll never forgive me. I can't say I've accepted it, though I do understand and I don't blame you. But I need you to know how sorry I am. I've been sober for three years. Met a guy at one of my meetings who conned me into going to church with him, too. I go every week now."

Jason shook his head. "Going to church doesn't—"

"I know. Church attendance doesn't mean anything, but you need to know that I don't go to impress. I'm not the same. I'm a new creation. The old has gone and the new has come. I still have a temper, but I don't make excuses for it anymore. I ask forgiveness.

I lean into grace. I've apologized to your mother, and to Richard."

Were those tears in his eyes? "I realize I'm the source of your worst memories. I'm not asking for a relationship with you. All I've wanted is for you to know that I am sorry and I do love you. Always have."

Jason's only response was a slow nod. Caroline hadn't realized she was holding her breath until she heard herself exhale.

Mr. Slater didn't seem to be worried about Jason's reaction to his apology. He straightened in the booth and turned his attention to Caroline. "If you decide you want to talk to William, or that you'd like for me to give him a call and ask a few questions, you know how to reach me."

His gaze made the circuit from Jason to Henry to Caroline and back to Jason. "You've got the makings of a nice little family here," he said with a sly wink. "I'll do anything I can to help you protect them."

Jason's skin flushed at his birth father's words. "Thank you, sir." The words sounded like they'd been ripped out of him, but there was a difference from before. The tone wasn't cordial, but it wasn't hostile, either.

Mr. Slater slid out of the booth. "Let me know."

"We will," Caroline said, her voice catching in her throat. She watched him walk away, then turned back to Jason. "Ready to go?"

He looked at her, and it took a second before he seemed to really see her. "Huh? Oh, yeah. Let's go." They grabbed refills and loaded back into the car in silence. The quiet stretched until they pulled into her driveway, when he reached for her hand. "I'm glad you were there for that," Jason said, his voice rough.

"I felt like such an intruder," she said.

"Never." He squeezed her hand. "I've been waiting twenty years for an apology from him. For some acknowledgment of wrongdoing. Mom's been begging me to accept his phone calls, but I've refused." He shook his head. "I'd convinced myself that I had forgiven him a long time ago. That I'd put it behind me. Of course, it was easier to believe that as long as he wasn't trying to get in touch with me." He put the car into Park. "Forgiveness is hard."

Oh, how well she knew it. "What he did was terrible."

"Yes, it was." He turned to face her. "Do you think people can really change?"

He needed more than a yes-or-no answer. How could she explain this to him? *Father, help me. Give me the words.* She paused a few seconds. This praying was happening more often. When had that happened?

"I do. I've seen it. Stephanie changed. When I went to Duke and she went to ASU, we drifted apart for a while. She made some bad choices, started partying, gave me a hard time for not being much fun to be around because I wouldn't get drunk with her." She hesitated to say the next part, but she had to. "When Chad died, she came right away. His death…"

She fought the tears that threatened. "I will never know why his life was so short, but his life mattered. And so did his death. I know of at least twenty people who came to Christ as a direct result of the sermon preached at his funeral. And Stephanie was never the same. She went back to church, sent me cards with Bible verses, prayed with me and for me."

She dropped her head. "When she told me she was pregnant, I'm afraid I didn't take it well. I always wondered if she'd really been married, or if she'd fallen back into bad habits and was ashamed to admit it." A tear escaped, and Jason's finger brushed it away. "But I know now that wasn't true. She never went back to the way she was. She'd been changed forever. So yeah, I believe people can change."

Jason seemed to be considering her words. "Did you believe him? My birth father?"

"I've heard some rumors," she said. "People are saying he's not the same. Dad told me he'd heard that your father lost a few clients because he wouldn't help them try to get around some legal issues the way they wanted him to. I've also heard he's in church. And when

I saw him at the Fultons' Christmas party, he was drinking water."

"It could have been vodka," Jason said.

"No. I was standing there when he ordered it."

"So you believe him? You think I should let it all go?"

"That's not what I said. I said I've heard he's changed. I think the issue of forgiveness is one you already know the answer to. The question isn't whether or not you should forgive him. The question is whether or not you think he deserves it."

"He doesn't."

"None of us do."

He huffed. "No. I guess we don't." He rubbed a circle on her hand.

She smiled at him. "You've been waiting on this for twenty years. Give yourself more than twenty minutes to process it."

He got out of the car and walked around to her side. When he opened the door, he took her hand as she climbed out. But instead of stepping back to give her some room, he put one hand on her waist.

Her eyes found his, and what she saw there made her heart fly. Was he going to kiss her again?

Henry's piercing wail shattered the moment, and they both laughed. Jason pulled Henry from his car seat. Caroline expected Henry to lunge for her, but he didn't. He tucked his head under Jason's chin and snuggled in, his eyes fluttering closed.

Jason shrugged. "He's a great little guy," he said.

They made their way into the empty house. Kyle must still be at the Crawfords' house, she figured. She took a little longer than necessary to get Henry ready for bed. She brushed the hair from his face after she pulled his pajamas over his head. He'd been a trouper. He'd endured so much.

When would it finally be over?

Father, do we have to call them? Do we have to make contact?

When the idea settled into her heart, the fear

that she'd expected to accompany it wasn't there. It was more of a certainty that God was in control and that she could trust Him. With Henry. With Jason. With her future.

She kissed Henry good-night and found Jason studying the monitors Kyle had left in her dining room.

"I think we need to make contact with the Larrabies but keep Henry's existence out of the picture," she said.

He nodded. "I agree, and I might have a way we can do it."

"How?"

"Heidi's been investigating the death of Charles Townsend, who we suspect was really Lee Baker. She's only a couple of hours' drive from the town where the Larrabies live. She could talk to William Larrabie about Lee and get a feel for his attitude toward him. Even ask him flat out about his kids if she has the opportunity."

"But keep Henry out of the conversation?"

"Of course," Jason said. "You should know

there's a chance that if we approach him and get him thinking and talking about his half brother, he might hire people who will put the pieces together the same way we have and find out about Henry. Then again, there's nothing to prevent him from doing that at any time in the future—and there's a good chance it's already been done, and that's how the twins found out, if they're the ones who have been behind the attacks. I'd rather be the one asking the questions and be ready for whatever might come than to get blindsided by a knock on the door down the road."

"That's a good point," she said.

"Do you want to call her, or shall I?"

She smiled. "You do it. You can be the supercop while I see if there's anything to eat in the house. At some point I'm seriously going to need to go to the grocery store."

"You didn't have enough at Hot Dog World?" He was laughing as he dialed the number. She stuck her tongue out at him and went into the kitchen.

She'd found some popcorn and a stash of frozen cookie dough and was making them a snack when he returned.

"Heidi's all over it. She's convinced Lee Baker is Larrabie's son. She talked to the clerk who married Stephanie and Lee. The wedding was legit. She thinks there will be enough DNA evidence either with his body or through Larrabie to get what we need to prove paternity if it comes to it."

"Okay." She wasn't sure she liked that, but she kept listening.

"She'll approach William Larrabie from the standpoint of someone who knew Lee and is seeking answers on his behalf. After she talks to him, we'll decide if it's worth asking my father to smooth the path toward the discussion about Henry."

Caroline's stomach flipped. *I'm trusting You, God. I'm trusting You.* She tried to smile.

"Don't worry," he said, obviously not fooled by her attempt to hide her turmoil. "We'll cross that bridge when we come to it."

Jason's phone rang. "Drake."

"Hi, Blake. Yes, she's right here."

He handed her the phone. "Blake, are you home?"

He ignored her question. "Where are you?" A lifetime of concern and big-brotherly affection colored his words.

"Home."

"Is that safe?"

"As safe as anywhere at the moment," she said. "Where are you?"

"Our flight was delayed. The weather here is horrible. We can't even hire a charter to get out. Everything is grounded. We may not make it back until tomorrow afternoon. I'm so sorry. I've been going out of my mind."

"It's okay," she said. "Jason's here."

"That does not make me feel better," he said. She could picture his face. He'd never liked Jason. Probably because he knew how much she did.

"He's saved my life several times," she said.

"Whatever," he said. She could tell he didn't want to fight with her at the moment. "Heidi called and filled me in. Dad knows William

Larrabie, so Heidi's going to be careful to keep all family connections out of her conversation. And I've left a message for Clark."

Clark? Her mind scrambled. Oh. Clark. The estate attorney. She had an appointment to talk to him next week about updating all her will and end-of-life documents as soon as the adoption was final.

"Why Clark?"

"Because I want him to confirm that there's no way anyone can legally claim Henry before we open that can of worms with Larrabie."

"Good idea. Thank you, Blake."

She heard a commotion, heard Blake speaking to Maggie. "I have to run. I'm so sorry. I should have been there with you. We're never all leaving again."

"Nonsense," she said. "This was beyond anything we could have anticipated. And I'm okay."

More commotion. "I have to go. I'll check in with you in the morning. Stay safe, Care Bear."

"I will. I love you."

"I love you."

She put the phone on the counter and checked on the cookies.

"He doesn't like me." Jason made the observation without any hostility.

"He doesn't know you very well," she said.

"My guess is that telling him I'm here as protector did nothing to ease his worries."

She hated that he was right. But he was.

"Don't worry about it," he said. "I always wanted an older brother like Blake."

"Get out of here."

"I'm serious." He took a bite of a cookie. "His loyalties are undivided. He doesn't care one bit about me—he only cares about you. About your happiness and well-being. And if I mess with either of those things, he will be sure to return the favor." He winked. "I always wanted someone who would look out for me that way."

She slid the remaining cookies onto a plate and set them on the counter. "So, now what do we do? I feel bad about the others still working so hard to try to salvage things at the Crawfords' house. Should we go back over there?"

"No. You are going to sleep. And so am I, for that matter. We both need it desperately. The next few days may be longer than the last few."

"You think someone's going to try to break in again?"

"No. I don't mean that. I mean emotionally trying."

She hated to admit that he was right. Again.

She yawned, and he laughed. "You've proved my point."

"It wasn't my fault," she said. "You were talking about sleeping. It was an unconscious reaction to the conversation."

He grinned but then contemplated her with a serious expression. "I'm not going to play games with you tonight, Caroline. No digging through Steph's old things. No laundry. No chores or tasks of any kind. You have to get sleep. Now. Tonight."

"I promise, but you have to promise to do the same," she said.

"I will. I'll call Michael and find out where our evening's protection detail is. As soon as they have things covered, I'll crash on your couch."

Three cookies and two handfuls of popcorn later, Caroline gave in to her exhaustion. "I guess I'll call it a night," she said.

"Sleep," he said. "Don't worry."

"Good night," she said.

When she closed the door to her room, all the strength left her body. She fumbled through her normal nighttime routine. Pajamas, face washed, contacts in solution, glasses by her bed. She'd thought it would be hard to fall asleep, but her body had reached its limit.

Things couldn't go on like this. She needed answers. She needed a plan. She needed to get her life back. Henry's life back.

She needed to be able to see where things were going with Jason and what that looked like.

Of course, she needed to be alive to do all of that, but no one had tried to kill her yesterday. That was something to be thankful for.

Father, continue to protect us. Show us what to do.

EIGHTEEN

"You have to be kidding me," Jason said. Caroline didn't appear to be joking, but she couldn't possibly be serious. Could she?

"I am not," she said as she spread cream cheese on a bagel. "I have work to do. Employees who are counting on me. No one else in the family is here. I have to go to work today."

"You do not have to go anywhere."

"I can't stay here forever, Jason. I have responsibilities."

"Someone is trying to kill you."

"You don't think I know that?"

He saw the way the knife shook as she placed it on the counter. He made an effort to keep his voice low and his tone calm. "Going to work isn't the answer."

"How do you know?"

"Because I know you don't want to endanger any of your employees and friends."

Caroline's shoulders sagged. "I have meetings..."

"They can wait."

"I'll need to make some phone calls." The words cracked, and she turned toward the refrigerator. "I guess I could make them from here."

"I think working from home is a great idea." It would help keep her mind occupied and help her feel like she had some control, which was probably the biggest aggravation eating at her right now.

He put a hand on her shoulder, and she turned to him, burying her face in his chest. As much as he hated seeing her this miserable, he couldn't deny the way his stomach flipped at her touch, or the way her trust in him made him want to protect her every day for the rest of his life.

"I'm sorry," she said as she pulled away.

"This waiting for them to try to kill us again is making me crazy."

"It's making all of us crazy, but look at it this way. We know so much more than we did this time yesterday, and exponentially more than we did forty-eight hours ago. We are so close to solving this. Hang on a little longer, okay?"

She flashed him a grim smile and returned to her bagel.

The rest of the day passed slowly. Both of them spent a lot of time on phones and laptops. Kyle had returned during the night, and he kept constant vigil over the monitors. They took turns playing with Henry. There was no way he was going to day care today.

Michael brought in Mexican food for lunch, and Jason's mom went to the grocery store and dropped off the essentials—coffee, milk, bread, frozen pizzas, crackers and more doughnuts. They could withstand a weeklong siege if it came down to it.

It had better not.

Around two thirty, Kyle yelled from the

other room. "Car coming up the driveway. You expecting anyone?"

"No."

Jason joined Caroline as they leaned over the computer. Kyle tapped the monitor. "Either of you recognize this car?"

A dark sedan flew up the road. "No. But they're taking the curves like a pro."

"Or like they know the road," Caroline said. The car pulled to a quick stop beside Kyle's Camaro.

Jason took a position near the front door, Kyle near the French doors. Both had their weapons drawn. Both had a clear view of the monitors and could see the scene outside. The car doors opened, and Jason could feel the tension flee the room as the driver stepped from the car. She was small, but something about the way she moved made him think she'd be fierce in a fight. The way she adjusted her shirt when she got out of the car made him think she had a weapon at her waistband. That and the curly hair meant she had to be Heidi Zimmerman Harrison.

A strikingly beautiful woman climbed from the backseat, and they both paused to wait for the man who'd exited the front passenger side. He wasn't sure who the woman was, but he assumed the guy was Heidi's partner, Max. There was an easy camaraderie between the trio, but even through the camera he could see how alert Heidi and Max were.

Kyle had already slid his gun back into the holster. Caroline smiled at Jason. "Come meet my sister-in-law," she said. They walked onto the porch as Heidi reached the top step. She pulled Caroline into a quick hug. "You could have warned us," Kyle said from behind them.

"Why on earth would I do that?" Heidi said with a laugh.

"Still trying to keep me on my toes?"

"I knew you would be," Heidi said. "I told Max we might need to get out of the car with our hands up. I figured you'd be ready to take us out." They all laughed, but the mood turned serious quickly.

Heidi glanced around. "Let's make our introductions inside, shall we?"

No one argued. Once inside, Heidi turned to him and extended her hand. "You must be Jason."

"And you must be Heidi."

Max stuck out his hand. "Max Jacobs. Pleasure to meet you," he said. Jason shook his hand. Firm grip. Intense eyes. This guy wasn't someone he'd want to mess with.

Another hand, this one far more gentle than either Heidi's or Max's, reached for his. "I'm Sara Elliot," she said.

He looked between the three of them, then back to Sara. "You're the psychologist?"

"Yes."

Interesting. Sara hadn't introduced herself as a doctor, although he knew from Caroline that she had multiple advanced degrees. Was that out of humility or was it part of how she disarmed people before she analyzed them? He'd have to spend more time around her to know for sure, but her laid-back demeanor seemed genuine.

"Where's Henry?" Max asked. "I haven't seen him in ages."

"You saw him last month," Caroline said.

"Yes, exactly—ages ago."

"You'll have to wait until later," Caroline said. "He's taking a nap."

"I'll go peek in on him. Make sure his room is secure," Max said as he headed down the hall.

"You'd better not wake him up," Caroline said, her threat clear.

"Yes, ma'am," he said with a laugh.

Heidi rolled her eyes. "Honestly, if we don't find him a wife soon—"

"I heard that," Max said.

Caroline and Heidi laughed. Jason couldn't help but notice that Sara didn't.

Caroline must have noticed, as well. "Are you here to evaluate me, Sara?"

Sara smiled. "Not necessarily, but I'm here if you'd like to talk."

Caroline nodded. "Thanks." She swallowed hard. "I might take you up on that."

Jason could sense how hard that statement had been for her, but it made him even more proud of the way she was handling herself.

She was tough, strong, resilient, and she had the good sense to realize she might need help processing everything. That made her even more amazing in his book.

Max reentered the room, and Caroline sat on the edge of the love seat. "As much as I'd love to have a nice long gabfest and catch up, I can't," she said. "Let's get to business. Bring us up to speed on what you've learned."

Caroline looked from Heidi, to Max, to Sara and then back to Heidi. What she saw terrified her. The first night she'd met Heidi, she'd been all business. Compassionate but professional and 100 percent focused on the threat.

Over the past eighteen months, she'd learned to recognize the different sides of her new sister-in-law. There was the relaxed, fun-loving Heidi. Granted, Heidi's version of relaxed was still armed and dangerous, but she laughed more and she didn't check her surroundings every ten seconds.

Then there was on-the-job Heidi. On-the-job Heidi had always intimidated Caroline a bit. Okay. More than a bit. But on-the-job Heidi didn't make nearly as many appearances when she was at home as she used to. Maybe that was why the difference was so frightening.

Heidi was worried.

And if Heidi was worried, she should be petrified.

Jason took a seat beside her. "So what do you know that we don't?"

"For starters, we believe that the Charles Townsend who was killed in a jail riot in Wilmington, North Carolina, was, in fact, Lee Baker."

Max pulled out a sheet of paper and handed it to her. It was a copy of a North Carolina driver's license. The photo matched the mug shot of Charles Townsend.

"Lee Baker was born in Raleigh, North Carolina, to an Amanda Baker. No father was listed on the birth certificate." Max handed her another sheet. "Amanda Baker worked as a nurse until a few months before her death four years ago."

Caroline handed the birth certificate and driver's license copies to Jason. "How did she die?" Jason asked.

Max handed over yet another sheet. "Heart attack."

She looked at Jason and saw the question in his eyes. She looked back at Max. "Do you believe it was really a heart attack?"

"There's no evidence of foul play, but given everything that's happened, we have to consider the possibility that her death may not have been from natural causes," Max said, his face grim.

"Amanda Baker was working in the Duke University Hospital thirty-three years ago when Frederick Larrabie had quadruple bypass surgery. It's possible they met there."

Heidi picked the story up again. "At the time, Frederick Larrabie was married to a Vanessa Jones. The Jones family had old tobacco money, and she was the only heir. Even though it wasn't as common as it is today, they had a prenuptial agreement. Divorce on the grounds of infidelity would have cost him everything. Vanessa would have gotten not only all of her own money, but most of his assets in the settlement."

Jason stacked the papers into a neat pile and put them on the coffee table. "This is matching up with Stephanie's account so far," he said.

Max pulled out another sheet of paper and handed it to them. "This one, we can thank Sara for," he said. She didn't appear to appreciate being given the credit. Clearly, the tension between Sara and Max hadn't improved since the last time she'd seen them together. She never had been able to figure out why the two people who Heidi considered her closest friends struggled to get along.

"It wasn't a big deal," Sara said. "I was happy to be useful."

"Sara went in and sweet-talked the clerk," Heidi said with a laugh. "Came out of the office ten minutes later with a copy of the marriage certificate."

Everyone laughed.

"She still won't tell us exactly how she did it."

Sara winked at Caroline. "Every girl has her secrets."

Caroline studied the paper. "This is Stephanie's marriage certificate?"

"Yes. To Lee Baker. They were married in a small courthouse on the coast of North Carolina. The clerk remembered them. Said they were adorable and clearly in love. She heard him tell Stephanie he was sorry she couldn't have a church wedding, and Stephanie told him she didn't need a church wedding. Just him."

That sounded like Stephanie. She'd always been a hopeless romantic. Caroline took a sip of her tea.

"Based on what we were able to piece together, Amanda Baker told Lee about his birth father prior to her death, but he wanted nothing to do with Frederick Larrabie."

"How do you know that?" Caroline took another sip of tea.

Heidi cut her eyes over at Sara, and she flushed. "Because William Larrabie told me."

NINETEEN

Caroline spilled tea all over her shirt. "What?"

Sara grinned. "We went to his office this morning," she said. "I introduced myself and asked for a word. I showed him the picture of Charles Townsend, with the name hidden of course, and asked him if he recognized the man."

Sara had met Henry's uncle? The questions bubbled up before she could stop them. "What did he say? Did you tell him about Henry? Was he nice?"

Sara held out a hand. "Of course I didn't mention Henry. And he was very nice. You may not want to hear this, but I think he genuinely hoped to find his brother and connect with him," she said. "Apparently he only found out about Lee when he saw the will after his father's death, but he's been trying to track him down ever since. He opened his desk drawer and pulled out a file with a stack of pictures of Lee from childhood through adulthood that he'd found in his father's personal belongings. He told us he'd hired an investigator, but that they had been unsuccessful."

"Did you tell him what happened to Lee?"

"I told him the truth. That I was part of an investigation looking into a possible murder in a coastal jail. When he realized Lee had been killed, he broke down. I'm certain he had no idea."

"We don't have proof of this," Heidi said, "but we suspect that the private investigator found Lee, but instead of telling William, he told Liam."

"Why?"

"We have a theory. Just hang on. We're getting there."

Sara picked up the story again. "William Larrabie was quite forthcoming with me," she said. "Based on what we talked about and what we found in court records, we've been able to determine that Freddie Larrabie did, in fact, include Lee Baker in his will. Because he didn't know where Lee was at the time of his death, the will stipulated that most of his assets and a large sum of his money all went to William."

Max pulled out a grainy photo from his stack. "This house, another property on the coast and a trust somewhere in the neighborhood of ten million dollars went to Lee."

"Ten million?"

"Yeah, and this is where it gets interesting," Heidi said. "The money is being managed by a local company in Raleigh. A company that does have some legit dealings for window dressing, but that we suspect is mostly a front for a large Central American gang that has moved into the East Coast."

"Okay. I still don't see how this could possibly be a motive to kill Henry."

"It's because of the gang," Jason said. "Larry said he was mixed up with a brutal gang. If they have control of that money, they wouldn't want to lose it. And if Henry was found—"

"The money would be turned over to him. Or to Caroline, for him."

"I still don't get it," Caroline said. "How would the gang have gotten control of the money in the first place? Mr. Slater said that Freddie Larrabie was an honest guy and he believed William was, as well. Why would they have entrusted the money to a crooked company to manage?"

"We are still digging, but right now it looks like the connection may be with William's son, Liam."

"Mr. Slater said Liam was a nightmare," Caroline said.

"That's an understatement," Max said. "Liam Larrabie has a serious gambling problem. At first we thought he might be trying to take Henry out in order to get his hands on the money he would inherit, but then we found out more about the terms of the will. Now we suspect he may have been influential in getting the trust in the hands of this particular management company so the gang would be able to control the funds."

Heidi's face was grim. "Like Max said, we are guessing at this point, but I've seen it before. Rich, spoiled kid starts playing around with some relatively minor criminal activity. Thinks he's immune to anything really bad happening to him, and then gets himself in over his head. These gangs don't play, and they wouldn't hesitate to force Liam Larrabie into a situation where he would do whatever they said just to stay alive."

Heidi paused a moment before she continued. "According to William, Liam began to have a much greater interest in the family's affairs after Freddie's death. We suspect it has more to do with protecting himself than really wanting to learn the business."

"So why don't we talk to him and ask him?" Caroline asked. "Don't you have enough to bring him in for questioning?"

"We would, but we ran into a bit of a problem there."

Caroline felt the nerves tingling along her arms. "What problem would that be?"

"Liam and Fern fled the country two days ago. Their passports were scanned in Croatia."

"Croatia?"

"It's a decent place to run to if you have plenty of cash. Nice beaches and no extradition policy with the US," Kyle said.

Caroline thought she might be sick. "Another dead end?"

"Yeah, but that's not the whole problem."

"There's more?"

Heidi nodded. "We were able to get a look at airport security camera feeds both at their departure point and arrival."

"How—" Jason began, but Heidi cut him off.

"Don't ask," she said with a wink. "The point is, we have a few photos of the two of them. And while Fern Larrabie is definitely in Croatia, we don't think she's with Liam. In fact, we suspect Liam never left the United States."

Max handed over a few more grainy photos.

"We ran the images through facial recognition software. That is definitely not Liam Larrabie. His name is Lance Smith and he has a rap sheet we could use to wallpaper your entire living room."

Dread settled in Caroline's stomach. "You mean…"

The look on Heidi's face confirmed her fears before she spoke. "He's created a fake alibi to cover his tracks. We don't know where he is."

TWENTY

Jason couldn't stand the look on Caroline's face. He reached for her hand, and she clung to it with far more force than he'd expected. The only reaction from the trio across from them was one quirked eyebrow from Max.

"We're looking for him," Heidi said. "I have people tracking his known associates. It's possible the gang had enough and took him out, but that's unlikely. It's more likely that they have told him to fix the situation with Henry, and if he doesn't, they'll make him pay."

Max leaned back on the sofa. "We have evidence of what these gangs are willing to do. They've tortured people. Most of them have ended up dead, but a few victims they left alive to spread the terror. They are not the kind of people you want to meet on a sunny

day in a crowded place, much less alone in your home after dark. The fact that you are alive is nothing short of astonishing. The guy they used must not have been too closely associated with the gang, or he would have made sure he killed you both the first night." While his words had been matter-of-fact, his eyes burned with compassion, maybe even pity.

"Jason," Heidi said. He focused on her, unsure of what she might say next. "Max's findings and assessment match up with the story your prisoner told you. Have you been able to confirm any of it?"

"I have. Haven't even had a chance to tell Caroline yet, but Larry does have an ex-wife and an eight-year-old son who's already had five heart surgeries. Our prisoner has a record, but he's been clean for twelve years. Looks like when they were faced with losing their house, he took out an ill-advised loan from an old buddy and then started gambling to try to pay it back. The buddy turned out to be gang affiliated."

Max was nodding. "Gangs don't exactly

offer a family-friendly payment plan. And a guy with a record? They'd want to make him use his skills to pay them back."

"Exactly," Jason said. "Larry was scared to death. He made it sound like he'd been hoping to do enough to keep them from coming after him or his family, but not enough to actually kill anyone."

He squeezed Caroline's hand tighter. "With Larry unable to finish the job, we have to try to anticipate what their next move will be."

"There's no way they'll let this go," Heidi said. "We're speculating here, but it's likely Liam made them believe this money would be available to them for a long time. Apparently the way the will was written, the money was to be held for fifty years. If Lee, or his heirs, hadn't come forward by that time, then the money would revert back to the other Larrabie heirs. It's a lot of money, and they aren't the type to relinquish it."

"And Liam is using that money to pay off his own debt to them?"

"It seems likely," Heidi agreed. "He probably insisted that the trust be managed by that company. And we suspect he bribed the investigator to give him the information on Lee, which he then turned over to the gang. They would have arranged for the arrest, the fake identification, and then for Lee to die in jail. By having him arrested under a false name, they could keep William Larrabie from stumbling across a random news report about his death.

"My guess is that Liam has no idea how bad this is. He will never be free of them, but they are probably stringing him along, telling him if he takes care of this little problem, that will be the end of it. They may even insist he take care of it himself. If he gets caught, it looks like he was after the money for his own personal use and their little enterprise could possibly carry on unobstructed."

"What if we get to him first?" Jason asked.

Heidi gestured for Max to take this question. "If he's willing to testify against the people he's involved with, he might have enough evidence to be able to land a spot in a witness protection program. He'd have to leave his family, his sister and definitely his lifestyle, but he'd be alive."

"Unfortunately," Heidi added, "he's either too stupid to realize he has the second option or too arrogant to realize he could be caught."

"So he's going to keep trying to kill me and Henry, even though killing us won't help him at all."

"Yep."

A heavy silence fell over the group. "What now?" Caroline asked. "I am not going to sit here and wait for someone to kill Henry, or me." She glanced around, and her eyes widened. "You shouldn't be here. Now that we know why I'm being attacked, you're all in danger for absolutely no reason at all." She stood up. "I'm serious. It's me and Henry they are after, but if you stay, you're putting yourselves in harm's way."

Was she out of her mind?

Heidi shook her head. Max sat back farther into the sofa. They both looked at him with expressions that said "She's nuts."

Sara stood and walked over to her. "Caroline," she said in a tone so calm and controlled it must be her professional voice, "if you think any of us are going anywhere, then you and I are going to need to spend some serious time together."

Caroline didn't smile. "I can't allow—"

"You are allowing nothing," Sara said. "Jason wouldn't leave you at this point no matter what you said. Heidi and Max don't think they've had a fulfilling day unless someone tried to kill them at least once."

Jason fought a smile. Heidi and Max had looks of fake indignation on their faces. They started murmuring to each other in stage whispers.

"Honestly," Heidi said.

"What does she know?" Max glared at Sara. "At least once. Please. It's not even worth getting out of bed for only one deadly encounter."

Caroline's lips formed an unwilling smile. She flopped back onto the love seat beside Jason. "Fine." She turned to him. "How do we end this?"

"Right now, almost all of our findings are circumstantial. It would be great if we could take down some heavy-hitters in the gang, but that's not our first priority. Our main goal is to protect you and Henry, so we are going to have to work on two different fronts. We'll explain our findings to William Larrabie and have the funds transferred to a different firm. It's possible that when they lose control of the finances, they'll stop trying to come after you. There'd really be no point in it for them."

"Okay. What's the other front?" Caroline asked.

"The other thing we have to do is find Liam," Jason said. "He's the one we believe set all of this into motion, and even if the gang can no longer get to the money, he may still want to see Henry eliminated so the money will go to him and Fern."

Even with nothing more than a few laptops, Heidi and Max had access to files and information that Jason could only dream about.

He'd called the sheriff and filled him in on

the latest developments. He wasn't surprised when he was told to stick close to Caroline and get to the bottom of this mess. The sheriff didn't mince words. "You take care of that girl," he said. "Jeffrey Harrison is one of my oldest friends. I've known Caroline since she was an infant. If anything happens to her or that little boy…"

Was he choked up? Jason held his breath until the other man cleared his throat. "You have permission to do whatever it takes. I'll free up as many resources as I can. Protection details, extra patrols, whatever we need to do."

"Yes, sir."

Kyle came and went a few times as he made what he called "upgrades" to the camera system that let them monitor most of the Harrisons' mountain.

As daylight faded, pizzas were delivered by two of Henderson County's finest. Everyone had agreed ordering takeout was asking for trouble. Better to have the food brought in by people they could trust. The officers stayed on-site, patrolling the property and keeping an eye out for intruders.

Everything was quiet until 8:43 p.m. when a car entered the driveway. They all walked to the porch and waited. When the driver exited the car, the difference that came over Heidi was so noticeable Jason had a hard time making sense of it.

The all-business FBI agent ran straight for the man. He scooped her in his arms and spun her around. The kiss he planted on her lasted so long Jason had to look away.

"Newlyweds," Max said under his breath. "I hope they get over this soon."

"I don't," Sara said, a wistful smile on her face.

"Me, neither." Caroline laced one arm through his. "They deserve it."

"Yes, they do," Kyle said. "But where's Maggie? I haven't seen her in ages."

"She's at her other grandparents. With round-the-clock security until this is over," Sara said.

"The agents Heidi called in were ecstatic

to get to hang out with Maggie again. They'll keep her safe," Max said.

They all made their way into the house. Jason looked over his shoulder and caught the moment Blake pressed his forehead to Heidi's. He held her face in his hands, and even in the dim light, Jason could see how much he treasured her. How precious she was to him. How he would do anything for her.

He patted Caroline's hand, still tucked in his arm. Could they ever share a bond like that?

Her eyes met his. Maybe. All the reasons he'd had for staying away when he was eighteen—his fear of never knowing when his birth father would show up and cause a scene, his worries about what kind of father *he* would be that left him convinced he should never have children, and even his certainty that Caroline would be better off without him but that he couldn't bear to see her with someone else— none of those reasons seemed valid any longer. Well, maybe they had been valid at the time, but they no longer seemed insurmountable.

Could he live with himself if he didn't at least try?

* * *

Caroline stepped back into the house, Jason by her side. Max and Sara followed immediately. She expected Heidi and Blake to linger on the porch, but they entered seconds later.

Blake made a beeline for Caroline. She stepped away from Jason and let Blake squeeze her so tight her lungs struggled to expand.

"I'm sorry you've had to go through this alone," he said in a whisper.

"I wasn't," she said.

Blake cut his eyes in Jason's direction. He didn't look thrilled with the idea of Jason being around all the time, but at least he kept things civil. He stuck his hand out, and Jason grasped it.

"Thank you for taking such good care of her," he said.

Jason dipped his head. "Not good enough."

"That's not how I heard it," Blake said with a glance in Heidi's direction. "If my wife approves, that's high praise. She's a tough one to impress."

"Ain't that the truth," Kyle said from his post at the dining room table.

Blake smiled. "She has a bit of a reputation," he said, pride coloring his words. "She expects people to do their jobs and do them well. She's very pleased with you."

"But the people after Caroline and Henry are still out there."

Blake ran his hand through his hair the way he did so often when he was frustrated. Heidi patted his arm. "We know who we're looking for now. That's a big improvement over where we were a few days ago."

Neither Jason nor Blake looked convinced, but whatever Heidi had said to Blake, it had been enough for Blake to be okay with Jason providing a level of protection for her. That didn't mean he would approve of him as a boyfriend.

Boyfriend?

Could she ever have a boyfriend again? With Henry in her life, did she have the luxury of dating someone to see how it worked out? Would it be fair to Henry to bring a man into his life she wasn't sure was there to stay?

No. It wouldn't. But did it matter? Now that Jason had reentered her life, would anyone else ever be enough?

This was crazy. Thinking this way when she had so many more important things to deal with. Like staying alive.

Blake looked around the room. "What's the plan?"

"We have every law enforcement agency in the country on the lookout," Heidi said. "Liam's passport is flagged, but given that he let someone else use it to leave the country, I don't see us getting very far with that."

"But we'll find him. He's not a pro. He'll mess up," Heidi said with her usual confidence.

Jason agreed. "I say tonight, we post guards and we sleep. Tomorrow, we follow the money."

Everyone nodded their agreement. "I like it," Blake said.

"Me, too," Heidi said.

"I like the sleep part the best," said Max with a wink in her direction.

"You would," said Sara with a disgusted shake of her head.

Jason's phone buzzed in his pocket. He glanced at the number. "Excuse me a moment."

He stepped onto the porch, and Caroline turned her attention back to the security plans Heidi and Kyle were discussing to ensure they all remained safe during the night.

Jason ran back into the house. "Caroline, can I have a word?" His ashen face drew her to him.

"What is it?" she demanded.

He held the door for her, and they walked onto the deck.

"Dad."

Her heart sank. "What happened?"

"He fell," he said, rubbing his lips together. "They're at the hospital. Doing a CT scan. He may have a concussion and might have broken his leg."

"Go," she said. "Go to them."

"I can't leave you alone."

"I'm not alone, but they are. Go. Stay with your mom and dad tonight. It's why you moved here in the first place. I'll text you every thirty minutes."

He was so clearly torn.

"Jason." She put her arms around him, and he clung to her. "This is your dad. You have to go. I'm sorry this has happened, but staying here won't do anything other than make us both feel guilty. Heidi, Max and Kyle will probably have a round-the-clock patrol set up by the time I get back in there. Henry and I won't be alone, and we'll be well protected."

He held her tight. "I'm sorry I can't be here for you."

"Don't feel bad for me. I'm just sorry your mom and dad are going through this."

His arms tightened around her. When they relaxed, she thought he was going to release her. Instead, his lips pressed into her hair. "I've missed you so much," he said.

TWENTY-ONE

"I've missed you, too," she said.

Oh, how he wanted to believe that. "When this is over—"

"You'll go back to pretending I don't exist?"

Ouch. "I have never been oblivious to your existence."

She snorted. "Only all my life."

"What is that supposed to mean? We were together almost every day until we graduated from high school." She didn't respond. Wait a minute. He pulled back. "You aren't serious?" That pink tint covered her face again.

He groaned. "Caroline, I've been in love with you since we were seven. How could you not have seen that?"

She took a step back and he let her, but he didn't let go of her completely. "You've what?"

Well, he'd done it now. What could he say?

"If that was love—" she sputtered.

"Like I had a chance."

"What is *that* supposed to mean?"

"You're Caroline Harrison. You could have any guy you wanted. I was just a poor kid from the wrong side of your mountain."

"You don't honestly believe that, do you?" Incredulity filled her face.

"I did."

"And now?"

"I still believe you can have any man you want."

She held his gaze. "That's not what I meant."

He shrugged. "I know you're too good for me. You always have been."

"What have I ever done to make you say that?"

"It's nothing you've ever done, or said. You're just... You're, well... You're you."

"That explains exactly nothing."

"You are beautiful, thoughtful, intelligent, caring, funny, adventurous, loyal. You do not have a single negative character trait." She watched him through narrowed eyes. "You have always been unattainable."

She shook her head. "No. When it comes to you, I have always been in reach. Always. If you've loved me since you were seven, why didn't you say so that night? I told you how I felt, and you told me you didn't feel the same way."

"I lied."

Her eyes glistened. "Why?"

"It seemed logical at the time. Everything that matters to you is here. Your family. Your business. Your life."

"But not you."

"I couldn't stay."

"I never expected you to," she said. "I kept hoping you'd ask me to come with you. And you never did. That night…" Yeah. That night. Their last night together before he left for the military. She'd kissed him. Told him she loved him. And he'd told her he didn't feel the same way. It had hurt her so badly that she'd cut all ties with him after that, refusing to speak to him when he'd tried later to reconnect.

This was a conversation long overdue. And even though there were big things for them to deal with, this one had to be dealt with now.

"I panicked."

She nodded slowly but didn't say anything.

"We…I…" He stopped. How could he ever explain it? *Get over yourself, Drake. If there's ever a hope of anything with her, you're going to have to get this out in the open.* He tried again. "For a few minutes, all I could think of was you. The way you felt in my arms. The way you tasted. The way you smelled. But then I thought about your dreams of living here on the top of this mountain, of running your family's business. Your life. Your family. And I convinced myself we would never have a chance. It was the most cowardly thing I have ever done. I regretted it the minute the words came out of my mouth. I could see the hurt on your face. I knew how much it had cost you to be honest with me, and I wanted to tell you the truth. But I convinced myself you'd be better off without me. So when you told me you never wanted to speak to me again, I decided the best thing for me to do was honor your request."

He couldn't tell if his apology was helping or hurting his cause. "I missed you so much, but I convinced myself that I was doing the right thing. That staying away from you was the most loving thing I could do. And then you moved on."

"Do you blame me?" she asked.

"Not for a second, but it proves my point. There are other men, better men, out there."

"I don't want them."

Did she really mean that?

She stared him down. Her face went from pink to deep red, but there was no hint of retreat in her expression. "I'm not going to say I've been sitting around pining after you, but for the past couple of years, you've been in my thoughts so often. I've prayed for you and wondered about you. Not that I ever thought there was any chance of you coming back, or us growing close again."

She squeezed her hands on his waist, and he had to fight to keep his own hands from finding their way to her face and pulling that sweet mouth to his.

"But I did miss you. Your friendship and your laughter and the way I felt whenever I was with you. I've wondered what the adult version of Jason Drake would be like."

He couldn't resist. "And what do you think of him?"

He could see it in her eyes. She wasn't going to let him turn this into a laughing matter.

"I see a man who gave up a career he loved so he could come take care of his dad and be there for his mom in the hard years ahead. I see a man who has literally risked his life to protect me and my son. I see a man who was willing to put himself in the debt of the one man he most wants to avoid, all so he could help me."

"You don't—"

"I'm not done," she said. "I see a man who never wanted to be a father but has a real knack for it. I see a man who is willing to at least consider forgiving a man who made his childhood something out of a horror movie. I see a man who is willing to own up to his mistakes." She lowered her gaze, and her voice dropped to a whisper. "I see the man I knew you would grow to be."

"I don't deserve you." How could she not see that?

"I'm not exactly a prize, Jason Drake."

"I think we've already covered my opinion of you."

She shook her head. "I'm now a single mom, and you never wanted children."

"I've been rethinking that position for a while," he admitted.

She narrowed her eyes. "Okay. I can believe that, but what about my job? I have a demanding career with people who count on me. I can't walk away from it."

"I would never ask you to leave."

She looked at him then. "So you'd leave me behind. Again?"

His hands found their way to her face, and he held her so she couldn't look away. "Never. Never again. There is nothing on this earth that could make me leave you." He brushed his lips across her forehead. "If I could make myself believe that you really wanted to be with me—"

Her lips found his. She was kissing him. His mind struggled with the implications. She wanted him? Did she? Could she? She pulled away slightly, her face the most lovely shade of pink he'd ever seen.

"If I didn't know better, I'd say you were trying to flirt with me."

She laughed. "Is it working?"

"You have no idea," he said as he pulled her face back to his.

Could this be happening?

Was she really kissing Jason Drake? Was he kissing her? After all this time, in the middle of all this chaos, was it possible that the deepest longings of her heart could be coming true?

Jason deepened the kiss, and she fell right over the edge. There was no coming back from this. No way to deny it. No matter what happened now, she couldn't pretend she didn't care.

She was in love with Jason Drake.

She hoped she lived long enough to enjoy it.

When he pulled away, he rested his forehead against hers. It was several moments before either of them spoke. "Caroline," Jason said, his voice thick with emotion. "I need to go."

"Okay," she said, not moving.

He looked at her, eyes wide and wondering. "When I get back, you may need to remind me that this wasn't all a dream."

"Let's not start that nonsense again," she said, trying to get him to smile. "You're stuck with me now."

"For better or worse," he said with a mischievous smile. His lips found hers before she could answer, but if he'd given her a chance, she would have said yes.

TWENTY-TWO

Jason drove his mom and dad home from the hospital at 11:30 p.m.

"I'm glad they didn't keep us there all night," his mom said from the backseat.

"I told you I was fine," his dad muttered from the passenger side. "Lots of worry over nothing."

"It wasn't nothing, Dad. You were bleeding and they thought you might have broken your leg."

"Head wounds always bleed a lot. I wasn't about to die. You didn't need to come rushing over there. You should have stayed with your girl."

"My girl is fine. I talked to her thirty minutes ago. She was going to bed. She's surrounded by FBI agents. I think she'll survive the night without me."

"Your girl?" his mom's voice piped up again from the backseat.

"Maybe," he said.

He tried to keep his voice neutral, but he knew he'd failed when his mom squealed like a little girl. "Praise the Lord," she said.

"'Bout time," his dad said.

"Don't go getting ahead of yourselves," he said.

He should probably take his own advice, but his heart wouldn't cooperate. As soon as he'd realized his dad's condition wasn't critical, Caroline had returned to the surface of his thoughts. He'd already planned their first real date. And the second. And the third.

"Earth to Jason," his dad said.

"Sorry," he said. What had he missed?

"I asked if you're any closer to finding out what's going on."

"We caught the guy who was in her house and we know who's behind the attacks."

"They aren't the same person?"

"No."

"So when you say you know who's behind the attacks, that means you know who it is but not *where* he is?"

"We'll find him."

"I have no doubt you will, son."

Jason wished he had his dad's confidence.

"You going back over there tonight?"

"No." He didn't want his dad to realize that he was staying because of him. The truth was he didn't want to leave them tonight. The doctors had said there was no concussion, but he didn't want to risk there being any trouble during the night and his mom needing help. "I think I could use a night in my own bed. I've been sleeping on a lot of couches lately."

"I think that's wise," his mom said from the backseat. "You can go back in the morning."

But when the morning dawned, he found himself needed at home. His dad's headache had worsened during the night, and his mom hadn't slept. Jason sent her back to bed and fixed breakfast for him and his dad. He tried to enjoy the quiet time, but it was difficult to relax. He knew Caroline was okay, and she was only a few minutes away, but he didn't like the distance between them.

His mom came into the kitchen around 11:00 a.m. "You need to get out of here," she said. "I'm fine. Get back over to Caroline's house."

"There's no rush, Mom."

His mother let out a little huff. "You don't actually expect me to buy that, do you? That girl is in danger. So is her son, and I've seen you with him—you can't pretend that precious boy hasn't stolen your heart, too. You have a nut job trying to kill the pair of them. Get back over there and solve this case so you can marry her. I've always wanted her for a daughter, and I'm not about to risk losing her now."

"Yes, ma'am," he said. He pecked her cheek before he sprinted for his car.

As he drove toward the house, he heard a sound he couldn't place. It almost sounded like a low-flying airplane, but cruising at that altitude over the mountains was a pretty stupid move.

He punched in the code to the Harrisons' driveway. The gate opened before him.

A moment later, the mountain shook.

He floored it.

He passed Blake's house, but as he approached Mr. and Mrs. Harrison's, he drove into what he first thought was fog but then realized was a mixture of smoke and debris. He couldn't see the road, so he left the car in the Harrisons' driveway and ran.

God, please. I can't lose her.

He pulled out his phone and called the dispatcher.

"There's been an explosion at the Harrisons'," he said. "We need ambulance, fire, rescue—everybody. And we need roadblocks. One-, five-, ten-mile radius. Maybe twenty-five." The closer to Caroline's house he ran, the harder it was to see. The harder it was to breathe. As he closed in, he had to dodge large chunks of debris. Parts of the mountain were catching on fire.

He rounded the final curve and skidded to a stop. The wind was blowing the smoke away from him now, and he could finally see.

Caroline's house was gone.

It took him a second to realize the ear-piercing cry was coming from his own throat.

He tried to absorb what he was seeing, but the horror of it dropped him to his knees. Stone and wood lay scattered everywhere. Bits of the forest that surrounded the house were smoking. A few small fires burned. The windows in the cars in the driveway had shattered, and all of the cars were destroyed.

In the distance, he heard the sirens. Help was coming. But what could they do? After such total destruction, what could anyone do?

He'd failed her.

He'd left her, again, when he said he wouldn't. And now she was gone. He'd lost her.

Again.

He fought to breathe. He didn't fight the tears streaming down his face.

His phone buzzed in his pocket again and

again, but he didn't answer. There was no one he wanted to talk to. The only person he'd give anything to speak to again was somewhere in that rubble.

But maybe... What if she had survived? What if she was buried in the debris?

As he ran toward the house, his phone buzzed again, and with it he felt a piercing sense of urgency. What if his mom had been trying to reach him?

He answered without looking at the screen. "Drake."

"Jason! Jason! Can you hear me?"

He must be dreaming.

"Jason. It's Caroline. I'm okay. Can you hear me?"

Hope flickered in his soul. Could it be? How?

"Caroline? Is that you?" *Father, thank You. Thank You. Thank You.*

"Yes!" Her laughter rang through the phone. "Oh, sweetie, I'm so sorry. We're all okay. We're in the safe room down in the basement. The sensors picked up the incoming projectile in time for us to head downstairs. We barely made it. But listen, Jason, this is important. Heidi says it may have been a drone with a bomb attached."

Jason tried to wrap his mind around what Caroline was saying. The pieces clicked into place. "I think it was, too. I heard something as I drove in. Thought it sounded like a low-flying plane."

"He heard something that sounded like a low-flying plane," Caroline said to someone near her. He could hear voices but couldn't catch what they were saying.

"Max and Kyle are into drones, and they say it would be hard to fly one that accurately without being nearby. The technology exists to use GPS markers and stuff like that, but that's only for really high-level stuff. Most drones the public can get their hands on require the pilot to be close." There was a pause as someone, maybe Kyle, rattled off something he couldn't catch.

"Kyle says either close or with a direct line

of sight. There are only a few houses higher than mine, so look up."

Close and high.

"Got it." He scanned the area as the smoke slowly cleared. Where would he be if he'd been flying a drone intended to blow up a house?

His thoughts scattered as a scrap of a curtain floated to the ground beside him. He still couldn't believe the house was gone. Almost everything Caroline owned had quite literally gone up in flames. Her heart would be so broken.

The weight of it all threatened to take him down.

Father, help me. Help me focus. Help me find him. Help me end this. And help me to trust that You will help us heal.

His phone rang again. "Drake," he said.

"Jason? Honey, are you all right? What happened?"

Jason slapped his palm to his forehead. How could he be such a moron? "Mom, I'm sorry.

I'm fine. I can't go into details right now. Caroline's house is destroyed."

"Oh, sweet Father, help us." His mother's prayer pulled moisture to his eyes.

"It's okay, everyone is fine—they realized what was happening in time to get to the safe room. We're hunting the guy now."

"How? Oh, never mind. Get that guy and then call me back."

"I will. But, Mom, stay in the house and tell Dad to keep the rifle handy, okay? I'm going to send one of the officers over to stay with you two."

"I don't need a babysitter."

"It's more for my benefit than yours."

She sighed. "Fine. I love you. Be careful."

Blake and Michael were running up the driveway toward him, but Michael was the first one to arrive. He stared at the house in horror, then clapped his hand on Jason's shoulder. "Dude, the dispatcher said Caroline Harrison called it in. She must be okay. But—"

"She is," Jason said. "She called me. They're in the safe room in the basement."

Michael's mouth dropped open in surprise. "Are you kidding me? Who has a safe room in their basement? Not that I'm complaining, but—"

Blake shrugged. "Heidi's idea. We all have one."

"Sure came in handy," Michael said. "This guy just won't quit, will he?"

How many lives had this idiot ended, endangered or damaged? It had to end. Now.

Firefighters arrived on the scene and started spraying everything down. The other police officers gathered around him, and they pulled out some topographical maps.

"What's the plan?" Michael asked.

"We're going on a hunch, but it's a solid theory and it's all we have to work with." He looked into the faces of the men whom he'd come to appreciate so much over the past six months.

"What did this?" Dalton asked.

"We think it was a drone fitted with a bomb. An experienced pilot could land one on a roof, or fly one through a window, and detonate it.

It's a huge national security issue. Our prime suspect has a known fascination for drones, and the security system caught something incoming. They had time to get to the safe room but not time to see what it was. I heard something that sounded like a low-flying plane on my way in."

"Sounds like a solid theory," Michael said. Heads nodded all around.

"Some drones can fly with GPS, but it would be tricky to do in these mountains and requires more tech than regular consumers can get. It's more likely he had to fly it in here by sight. Which means he's close. He could be on this property, but it's more likely he's nearby at a higher elevation. If he has a line of sight to the house, then he might be able to see us coming."

He made eye contact with each person. "This man has shown no hesitation to kill. He's not a professional, but he's determined— and callous enough to target a baby without hesitation or remorse. Use extreme caution."

Somber faces looked at the destruction around them. Their faces hardened.

Jason's phone rang. "Caroline, is everything okay?"

"We're fine. Listen. Is Blake out there?"

"Yes."

"Good. Ask him to point you to the Phillips' house. They're up on the next mountain. A little higher than mine. They're snowbirds and they don't usually come back to the mountains until May or June, but Sunday I thought I saw a light up there. In all the craziness, I dismissed it. Figured it was one of their kids checking on something for them before they came back. But it would be a good place to start."

"Got it." He slid the phone in his pocket.

"How do we get to the Phillips' house?" he asked Blake.

"There's an old dirt road behind the plant that will get you close and shouldn't be easy to see."

"Let's go."

Blake pulled Jason to the side. "I know how you feel about Caroline. I can see it on your face. And we had a long talk last night, so I know how she feels about you. I promise to keep her safe for both of us. You go get this guy so we can put all this behind us."

Jason nodded.

Blake pointed out the road on the map, and they took off. The next fifteen minutes passed in a flurry of activity. Roads had been blocked. Photos had been sent out. Anyone suspicious was to be detained.

They flew up the gravel road. As Blake had indicated, it dumped them out at the backside of the Phillips' property.

It was empty.

They could tell he'd been here from various bits of debris he'd left behind. Crime scene techs would scour the place, but they had enough evidence, and the line of sight was straight to the remains of Caroline's smoking house. Landing a drone on her roof would have been an easy exercise for anyone with a reasonable amount of drone-flying experience.

But Liam was long gone.

Phones and radios started squawking. One of the roadblocks reported a late-model SUV had turned around and flown back up the road it had come from after seeing the barricade. Officers were in pursuit.

They left a few officers at the Phillips' in case he returned, and everyone else took off down the main road.

"Black Escalade. 2016 model. Heavy mud on the tires. Didn't see anyone else in the vehicle, but the windows are heavily tinted."

"Officers in pursuit."

"Headed up Dupont Road."

Jason whipped his car around. If he could get there fast enough—

He floored it. Michael stayed with him.

Three minutes later he parked his Explorer smack in the middle of the road. Michael mirrored him.

"I had no idea this road even existed," Michael said as he hopped out of his car. You had to love a friend who would follow you first and ask questions later.

Jason grinned. "Yeah. Helps to have grown up on this little section of mountain."

"Officers still in pursuit," the dispatcher's voice squawked over the radio.

"Got to be getting close," Michael said as he dug around for something in the back of his car. He pulled out some spikes.

Jason raised a brow. "You drive around with those in your car?"

"I have for the past couple of days," Michael said. "Want to be prepared for anything."

They laid the spikes out thirty feet from their cars.

"Let's get out of the road. No sense getting run over," Michael said.

Jason looked at their cars but knew the vehicles were expendable. He and Michael took up positions on the sides of the road and waited.

One minute. Then two.

What if he'd been wrong?

Finally. Sirens screaming up the mountain. Tires squealing around curves.

He'd already confirmed with the dispatcher that there was no one else on the road who could get tripped up in their makeshift blockade.

"Here he comes," Michael shouted.

Jason watched, his weapon out. Michael had

a shotgun. Good choice for blowing holes in tires and vehicles without, hopefully, killing the driver.

Because despite everything, he didn't want this guy dead.

He wanted him alive so he could answer for his crimes.

The vehicle sped up the mountain and hit the spikes at full speed. The fancy tires held up to the impact pretty well, but the Escalade still fishtailed on the narrow road. Time seemed to slow as the car swung widely and approached their roadblock. Jason recognized the face through the windshield, and he watched in horror as Liam Larrabie pulled hard on the wheel and the Escalade flipped.

Once. Twice. And over the side of the mountain.

TWENTY-THREE

Caroline paced the small room. It had seemed like such a ridiculous extravagance when Heidi had insisted on the construction of a safe room last year. Her house, her parents' house and the bungalow Heidi shared with Blake and Maggie all now had their very own safe rooms.

She'd been sure Blake was just indulging his bride-to-be, but in this moment she was thankful she'd gone along with it.

Max leaned in one corner, bouncing Henry in his arms. Heidi and Sara conferred over something in another. Kyle kept grumbling about the reception and complaining about the now absent Wi-Fi signal.

What did he expect? Something had blown up her house. It seemed likely the modem was long gone. She leaned her head against the cool steel wall as her mind flitted from gratitude to terror, with maybe a little righteous anger thrown in.

She was alive. Henry was alive and would never remember the terror of the moment when Kyle told them all to run. But she would. She'd never forget the way her hand shook on the basement door. The way Kyle and Max waited until they were all inside before they closed the entrance.

The way the room shuddered violently four seconds later.

So close.

Too close.

But they were alive.

And whoever had done this was in big trouble.

Because the anguish in Jason's voice had turned to cold hard fury once he realized she was okay.

Father, don't let him kill anyone in anger.

Of course, she wanted Liam Larrabie

caught. Wanted him arrested, tried and incarcerated for a very long time.

Righteous anger tried to take over. Her house had been destroyed. Yes, the room had worked, and Heidi did have a bit of a smug glow emanating from her at the moment, but it never should have been necessary. How could money make anyone so crazy? How could they get to a place where killing innocent people was acceptable?

The craziest and most ridiculous irony of it all was that the more she thought about it, the more she knew that when the time came, she would ask William Larrabie to keep the money. He could set some aside for Henry if he wanted to, maybe enough for college. But she'd much prefer he put the bulk of whatever Henry's share would have been into charities that supported single mothers.

Money had its place and purpose, of course. She'd never known a time in her life when she didn't have plenty, and she knew there were situations and choices she couldn't fully grasp because of that. But too much money?

Sitting here in a safe room under the remains of her home, all she could see was that too much money made some people lose their minds. So, no, thank you. She didn't want that for her. She certainly didn't want it for Henry.

Would Jason agree?

That, she couldn't be sure of.

She must have dozed off, because the sounds of voices and heavy equipment first reached through her dreams. It took her a few moments to clear her head.

Those sounds weren't the sounds of a mountain slide. They were the sounds of her rescue. And apparently the only way she'd be rescued was if a crew dug her out.

"My house is completely gone, isn't it?"

She looked around the room. Grave expressions answered her.

She'd known it, but somehow she'd hoped at least some of it had been spared.

Heidi and Sara exchanged a loaded look, which Heidi then passed on to Kyle. He cleared his throat and walked over to her, iPad in hand.

"I used my phone as a hotspot and managed to tap into a camera that wasn't destroyed in the blast," he said.

He pulled up the feed and handed her the tablet.

She stared at it, uncomprehending. What was that pile of dirt? Was that Kyle's Camaro with— "Kyle, your car."

"It's just a car. I have insurance."

Max snorted. "Can't wait to see the claim on that one. I wonder if they'll try to get out of paying it by saying you aren't covered for drone strikes."

"Very funny," Kyle grumbled.

Caroline scanned the screen. A bulldozer of some kind pulled chunks of bricks and drywall over to a growing pile on the side of what used to be her house.

She stared at it. It was gone. Everything was gone. Her dishes, her souvenirs, her photographs. Everything she'd kept, from the candles on her sixteenth birthday cake to the bracelet her daddy gave her on her tenth birthday.

Gone.

She looked up, unable to hide the tears splashing onto the screen. Everyone was staring at the floor. Sara made eye contact first. Figured. She was used to walking through people's grief with them.

Caroline had no words. No way to express the sense of loss and anger she felt at those who'd taken her home. Mixed in was the realization that they'd been unable to take the things that mattered. Her family was alive. Jason was alive. Henry was alive.

The rest of it was just stuff. She'd told Jason that all those years ago, that the only difference between his lifestyle and hers was just stuff and it didn't matter to her.

Now she'd get the chance to prove it.

But boy, the loss of all that stuff?

It really hurt.

"Good thing none of us are claustrophobic," Kyle said.

"Speak for yourself," Sara said.

"What?" Max stared at her like he'd never seen her before.

She shrugged. "I don't like small spaces."

Max and Heidi shared a look. "She'd have hated—"

"That's exactly what I was thinking!" They shared a low chuckle.

"So glad I can be the source of so much amusement." Sara spoke with no trace of humor.

Heidi bumped Sara's shoulder with her own. "Sorry, it's—"

Four voices spoke at once. "Classified."

Then they were all laughing.

Caroline laughed right along with them, and the vise grip around her heart loosened.

Sure, it hurt. It would hurt for a long time.

But they were all going to be okay.

Jason and Blake were standing there when the safe room door was opened. Both of them rushed in.

Jason threw his arms around her and buried his face against her neck. She felt the dampness of his tears, and she clung to him, her own tears falling freely.

"You're okay," he whispered in her ear.

"So are you," she whispered back.

When his lips found hers, she didn't care they had an audience. She barely knew they were there.

This was all she needed.

All she would ever need.

This man, her son. Her family and friends by her side. This was what mattered.

The rest of it was just stuff she could live without.

TWENTY-FOUR

Three months later

Caroline looked up from her desk at Harrison Plastics International and scanned her calendar. For the first time in weeks, there were no court appointments to dread.

Liam Larrabie had survived his tumble down the mountain, but he had been in the hospital for over a month, during which time he'd proved to be an absolute pain to everyone who came near him. When he realized he was headed to prison for a long time, and that the gang would be able to get to him there, he'd agreed to testify against them in exchange for a new identity. His testimony had led to some high-profile gang arrests.

That was a story that would never be completely finished, but at least for now, there were no new pages being written.

Mr. Slater had brought William Larrabie to meet Henry and was helping sort through all the legal issues related to the estate and trust. Jason still didn't completely trust Mr. Slater, but they could be in the same room together for several hours, and every now and then Jason would smile or even laugh.

Some kinds of forgiving were slow processes, but they were moving forward in a direction none of them could have anticipated. The Larrabies had not objected to Caroline keeping Henry and had been able to provide DNA evidence to prove the identity of Henry's father, which had fully cleared the way for the adoption to go through. Henry was now 100 percent hers.

Everything had ended either well or as well as could be expected.

Caroline pulled her to-do list out and was trying to prioritize it when their office manager, Bridget, walked into her office carrying an enormous bouquet of candy bars.

"Looks like someone is trying to sweeten you up," she said with a wink.

Caroline pulled out the card.

Play hooky with me today?

Today?

She glanced at her calendar. She didn't have any meetings...

She jumped from her chair and ran into Blake's office without knocking.

"Hey," he said.

"Hey. So, um, I think I'm going to take the rest of the day off," she said.

Blake glanced at his watch. "It's nine forty-five."

"Yeah."

How could she explain?

The way Blake's mouth twitched made her think she wouldn't have to.

"Go," he said. "Have fun."

She ran around his desk and hugged him. "Thanks," she said.

"Love you," he called to her as she ran out of the room.

When she got to her car, Jason was waiting. "I wasn't sure you'd come," he said as he handed her a large iced coffee. "But I checked your calendar last night and it looked clear, so I thought I'd take a chance."

"You like checking people's calendars, don't you?"

"Do you mind?"

"Not at all. What are we doing?"

"Whatever you'd like to do," he said.

She climbed into his car. What would she like to do? It was not like she could go home. For now, she and Henry had moved back in with her parents. They'd finally cleared away the last of the debris from the remains of her house and declared the area ready to build on, again, but Caroline had been frozen in indecision about the next step.

Mainly because of the guy sitting next to her.

He winked at her. "Trust me?"

"Of course."

He pulled the car out of the HPI parking lot, and then a half mile later, he pulled into her driveway. They wound up to the top. To where her house had stood.

He got out and came around to open her door. He took her hand as she exited the car, and he kept it as they walked.

Caroline had a feeling she might know what was going on. Could he feel her trembling?

They got to their spot.

The one they'd shared their first kiss on, fourteen years ago. Her mouth went dry when she realized it was fourteen years ago. To. The. Day.

He pulled her into his arms. "I want to talk to you," he said.

"Okay."

He smiled. The smile that had always been for her and her alone. The one that said "I know you and I like what I know about you."

"Fourteen years ago, I ran away. I ran from you. I ran from my birth father. I ran from anything that might have required me to face up to my fears and my shortcomings."

"Jason—"

He placed a finger over her lips. "I'm never going to do that again. I love you, Caroline Harrison. I've loved you since we were seven years old. I've loved you every day and I've wondered about you every day and I've regretted leaving every day. So, today, I'm asking you for another chance. A do-over. A fresh start." He looked at the cleared land. "We could rebuild our lives. Right here. Together."

He kissed her forehead. "This mountain—" he looked around them "—it's my home, too. I can't imagine a better place to raise a family. So close to both the grandparents and cousins for Henry, and any other children we have together. I'm in love with you. I adore you. I want to spend the rest of my life with you." He dropped to one knee and pulled a ring from his pocket. "Caroline Harrison, will you marry me?"

Caroline stared into his eyes and saw everything she'd ever longed to find there. Maturity, commitment, love.

"Yes." She tried to say it calmly, but the joy bubbled up and she couldn't stop the laughter that came with it. "Yes, yes, yes!"

He grinned and rose to his feet. "So, when do you think we might be able to do this?"

He kissed her before she had a chance to reply. A kiss that didn't change her answer but only served to confirm it.

"Soon."

* * * * *

Don't forget to check out
Lynn Huggins Blackburn's
first heart-stopping story

COVERT JUSTICE

Find this and other great reads at
www.LoveInspired.com

Dear Reader,

I've been looking forward to sharing Caroline's story since she appeared in my first book, *Covert Justice*. I hope you enjoyed Caroline and Jason's journey to forgiveness and love.

Caroline's life hasn't turned out the way she thought it would, and she's had to wrestle with whether or not she can trust a God who would allow some of the things that have come into her life.

Jason's childhood was marred with difficult relationships that have affected the choices he's made as an adult. He's had to find a way to get past them and begin the process of forgiveness.

I think most of us have had similar experiences. Ultimately, we know God is in control, but we still struggle when difficulties come our way. Sometimes we blame Him or turn away from Him. When we do, I'm so thankful that He understands when we doubt His goodness. He's a wonderful Father and is eager to receive us when we turn back to Him.

I'd love to hear your story of God's faithfulness to you. You can connect with me on social media or via my website at www.lynnhugginsblackburn.com.

Grace and peace,
Lynn